an
HONEST GHOST

D1241920

A NOVEL BY rick
whitaker

An Honest Ghost

a novel by

Rick Whitaker

Jaded Ibis Press
sustainable literature by digital means™
an imprint of Jaded Ibis Productions

COPYRIGHTED MATERIAL

© 2013 copyright by Rick Whitaker

First edition. All rights reserved.

ISBN: 978-1-937543-38-9

Library of Congress Control Number: 2013943178

Printed in the United States of America. No part of
this book may be used or reproduced in any manner
whatsoever without written permission from the
publisher, except in the case of brief quotations embodied
in critical articles and reviews. For information please
email: questions@jadedibisproductions.com

Published by Jaded Ibis Press, *sustainable literature by digital
means*™ An imprint of Jaded Ibis Productions, LLC, Seattle,
Washington USA

Cover and interior design by Debra Di Blasi.

This book is available in multiple editions and
formats. Visit our website for more information:
jadedibisproductions.com

for
David Whitaker

Happiness is an imaginary condition, formerly often attributed by the living to the dead, now usually attributed by adults to children, and by children to adults.

[The complete list of attributions begins on page 136.]

ℬ 1 ℭ

I am unpacking my library. I have been able to start work again on my novel. It is growing very slowly. There are limits to what can be said. Life lived by quotations.

You go back into your mind. The subjective universe.

There was an overflow of books on the floor, and on the coffee table I noticed a copy of Simone Weil's essays. It seemed neither appropriate nor necessary to David that he should get out of bed. "How can you do all that before coffee?" he asked through a yawn. He was twenty-four, and handsome in the way that makes young Englishmen, when they are handsome at all, the handsomest young men in the world.

At the moment, this romance is happy.

David said, "I keep reading about tribes or hordes of peoples who came sweeping out of Central Asia." My splendid David! My daily recreational activity. "What color were the Huns?" David said.

Our little love affair began one Monday afternoon when I received a telegram from Paris signed, so help me, Madame Marquis.

"Oh! How long shall we have to wait for the resolution of the chord?"

Well! I was dealing with a dangerous man who at any moment might burst into a selection from "The Paul McCartney Songbook." He was really sexy though; he was like a vast swimming pool I wanted to dive right into. I wrote in my notebook that meeting him I felt like Hazlitt meeting Coleridge for the first time: bowled over by his warmth and energy. There was something rather "doggy," rather smart, rather 'cute and shrewd, and something warm, and something slightly contemptible about him. To be in his company, to hold his hand, to feel his large fingers tighten round my own, made me feel very humble, very fortunate, very chosen. Sometimes he purred. He often pretended he was eating me. The action signaled his love of the illicit, his need to infect the scene with the fumes of a mésaliance.

I could spare him the time as my affairs were, surprisingly, rather stagnant at the moment. I would lie in bed every morning reading Cicero. I have never married, I have always lived quietly, and, apart from my interest in dahlias, I have no hobby. A few years ago I was a lawyer in Paris and, indeed, a rather well-known lawyer. I lived in the most serene, most chaste of surroundings. It was very agreeable in the springtime, with the chestnuts in the Champs Élysées in bloom and the light in the streets so gay. These arrangements turned me into a penniless dandy. Few men have the divine grace of cosmopolitanism in its entirety; but all can acquire it in different degrees. Occasionally I had nightmares, but in those days just about everybody had nightmares from time to time, though some more often than others.

David frowned. He was not well: he was a walking horror. It had been a difficult summer. When his friends asked what was going on, he remained silent or replied with some quote from his beloved Oscar Wilde, but even his characteristic wit had grown sluggish, and those quips, delivered so despondently, provoked only puzzlement and pity. His irony, intended to arouse sympathy, backfired. Prodded by his conscience, he began to generalize. Once, when I asked him how he was doing, he said he was always terrified. His rage had no one cause, not that he could discover, but bubbled up, a poisonous vapour, out of a mess of boiling emotions. The most innocent-seeming stranger, or even someone he thought he knew, might suddenly by a look, a word, deliver the secret message: *beware*. Cops always questioned him, though he never did anything wrong.

His early childhood was happy, but when he was six his parents separated and three years later his mother married a man whom her son would come to loathe. He was a balding, somewhat overweight, nervous man in his early forties. He died of a brain tumor in 1999. He lived a brief, passionate, unhappy life. Shall I describe the arrangements of their home life at this time? I found it hard at first to disguise the contempt which they inspired in me, but gradually I became accustomed to their way of life.

His mother had mental problems. After one first disappointment she had taken leave of the major emotions. She attended to the nearest matter at hand, no matter how trivial it was. The immense accretion of flesh which had descended on her in middle life like a flood of lava on a doomed city had changed her from a plump active little woman with a neatly-turned foot and ankle into something as vast and august as a natural phenomenon. She could be

Rick Whitaker

mistaken for a drag queen. She drank, she aged, she suffered terribly from her dissipations. Her clothes seemed to be all darts and buttons fastened mostly to show what they could not entirely contain. She had a fancy for tiny ivory or jade elephants; she said they were luck; she left a trail of tiny elephants wherever she went; and she went hurriedly and gasping. Her family, her husbands, her son, would have crushed any other woman I have ever known. David admires her prodigiously; he thinks her so good that she will be able to get him into heaven, however naughty he is.

How tender people are towards oppressors and how inexorable towards the oppressed!

"I'm rough and tough," she said.

One often makes a remark and only later sees *how* true it is.

"What a sweet pair of fairies you guys are," she said. Her voice was as hypnotic as a tom-tom, and as monotonous. I will not be commanded, she thought.

David leaned my way to fix me with a sad-eyed look. He was stretched out on his little mattress, and I noticed he had exchanged his dinner jacket for an embroidered kimono and was displaying the affected ease of the opium smoker. He puts on a queer smile. If there is *mésalliance*, as for the purists there must be, it was there from the start.

Though he was both rich and young, he knew how to control his passions. Even more commendable was his attitude to women, for he never pretended to scorn them and never boasted of his conquests. Very quickly, he discovered all the tricks of love: but being such a natural at them, he became entangled in the very love that caused them.

He talked incessantly about himself, yet was such good company that one could listen to the story of his ague forever. He was adequately vicious to stand apart from the rest of the world without being aggressive or disagreeable, save on rare occasions. Flushed with his impassioned gibberish he saw himself standing alone on the last barrier of civilization. I've been told so often that I would be helpless without him that I am slightly inclined to believe it, but only slightly.

David recalled dimly that he was getting drunk again, as usual, he reasoned, to escape. Not that there was much happiness in a life of pleasure. That is how it is: life, tight-buttoned life, fits him ill, making him too much aware of himself and what he glumly takes to be his unalterable littleness of spirit. He spent his life fleeing boredom, and he had no real goal beyond that.

A bell beat faintly very far away.

Although none of the rules for becoming more alive is valid, it is healthy to keep on formulating them. I am interested in wisdom. But it could hardly be otherwise. Some of my best friends are pedants.

It is impossible to return to the state of mind in which these sentences originated. Today is not like yesterday.

I swear I have rarely felt saner. But what kind of soundness is sanity? We long for a little weakness, darkness, and fiction, for the crowded, the smut, the closeness and malice of things. Life and death and death and life.

I believe in doing what I can, in crying when I must, in laughing when I choose. My life is all downhill. I live in my mind. (Like Holden Caulfield, I don't know exactly what I mean, but I mean it.)

All of us, even when we think we have noted every tiny detail, resort to set pieces which have already been staged often enough by others. The Zen masters have the saying, "Examine the living words and not the dead ones."

All work is the avoidance of harder work.

Shall we make war or shall we make peace?

The story that I am about to tell, a story born in doubt and perplexity, has only the misfortune (some call it the fortune) of being true: it was recorded by the hands of honorable people and reliable witnesses. To say that the story is true is by now a convention of every fantastic tale; mine, nevertheless, *is* true.

This is my own story, told in different voices. Not my usual method of composition.

೮ 2 ೞ

Day before yesterday was my birthday and I spent most of the evening sitting outdoors in the half moonlight informing two Brazilian intellectuals why they really should read Edmund Wilson, say, instead of Henry Miller, to get an adequate idea of U.S. letters. I got drunk, for the first time in ages I was really drunk again. I wasn't good for much at the age of forty, but I could drink bourbon and I knew which bourbon I liked and how I liked it. That was about it. Soon I'd be too old to attract anyone.

I took a terrace walk and saw the most brilliant falling star—I always make the same wish: Love. A black man was waving his arms and vociferating. The world to us was a perverse bestial and perverse philosophical plague and repulsive operetta. A part of drunkenness is the thinking that oneself is not sober. I didn't want to know what I was doing. I was amazed and confused. I was lost. Loneliness rose to the surface.

When I got home that night, I mean barely inside the door of my apartment, I heard these horrendous clunk-clunk-clunk footsteps coming up the stairs. A sound of hobnailed boots? Who comes here? Sometimes a venturesome sailor would stumble in, scary but irresistible. (O the weakness of human reason!) Still, the only thing worse than not getting it any more would be not wanting it any more.

Ding-dong.

Rick Whitaker

A minute later, a little kid appeared dragging behind him a small sailboat on wheels. I blushed intensely. Moving, as I do, in what would kindly be called artistic circles, children are an infrequent occurrence.

The child was small, a boy, and sad.

We shook hands, he looked at me with bright round black eyes that reminded me of someone I knew well. He seemed bloodless.

I was all ears.

Silence.

The uncertainty lasted only seconds.

I would not change the beginning for anything.

There are only a few shimmering moments in a man's life; all the rest is a dull gray.

A shiver ran down my spine.

It was a pale, sulky, painfully beautiful face. He looked extremely well fed and sane and clean.

"Joe, how are you, Joe?"

The visitor glided in and the door closed.

He gives me an odd little squeeze around the neck, his

face turning away from me. "I haf someding vich it is to ask you." He looked at me quickly and laughed, but so good-naturedly that I could not help smiling back at him. "Please answer me quite frankly. How can I live without you, wretched and unhappy as I am?" The question was asked with melancholy irony.

I do not know what to do.

I don't want to be one of those people weighed down by the suffering of humanity.

Absolute silence.

"And besides, don't be excruciating."

This is a strange outburst. "Well well well well well well. Unconditional surrender. Is that right?"

"You bet!" Joe said. "No harm in trying," he said. "I guess some people can't help doing the wrong thing." He noticed then that an internal obstacle, overcome, had passed away.

"Don't worry," I said. "Daddy was talking nonsense," I said with my brain whirling. "Your father is a fool, darling, and an idiot." This was all I said, though I was abundantly aware I needed to elaborate. "I am the opposite of you," I said.

"I like your simplicity," he said. "De bargain it is struck?"

It was the end of the first act of my life.

One is always somewhat in the dark in these matters; as much about one's own feelings as the other person's, and a certain amount of trial and error is inevitable.

All was greyness, without direction, with no above or below, nature in a process of dissolution, in a state of pure dementia.

"I haven't figured out what I want to be," he told me. "But you really must have a haircut, Father."

And so we find ourselves contemplating the future.

Phew!

That night, after finally falling asleep, I had a really sad dream. The twilight desert in my dream was thoroughly arid, and my tears dried even before they welled up in my eyes. What does this mean?

The rain beat against the window panes all night.

All night long, bad dreams sweep through me like water through a fish's gills.

The dream is incomparably stronger than the dreamer. The lamp is more important than the lamp-lighter.

ℬ 3 ℭ

But whirligig Time restores gaudy Aurora. I awoke, yet I dreamed still. Lost in darkness and confusion. Living with a precocious son is a father's worst nightmare. The first three days are the worst, they say, but it's been two weeks, and I'm still waiting for those first three days to be over. My artistic nature is going to degenerate, and my entire self with it. It was my nervousness, my very anxiety to know for sure what life meant, that made me rush through life in a perpetual state of worry. Suspense is fascinating—when it concerns what is happening to someone else. It is fear that I am most afraid of.

I regret sometimes not allowing the woman within me to express herself enough. The taboo gives us pause. But most men regard their life as a poem that women threaten. Fear tweaks the vagus nerve. So David tells me. Naturally.

Though blue, the sky had a dull sheen that was softening as the light declined. Very strange. To look at something which is "empty" is still to be looking, still to be seeing something—if only the ghosts of one's own expectations.

ଓ 4 ଓଷ

"I suppose my thoughts are nothing to be proud of," said Eleanor Sullivan. "I know you like poetry."

From the first moment ours was a *spiritual* friendship.

"I wonder why people say that in such a contented tone," said Eleanor. She sounded slightly bitter, almost irritated. Few emotions are harder to repress than resentment. Her voice softened, almost singing. She was capable of drinking too much. "Oh, well-behaved—that's a whole way of life, isn't it?" A hard-bitten cruel-mouthed adventuress. She's insane and insatiable. At this very moment, no doubt, she is pondering with regret decisions made in the far-off past that have now left her, deep in middle age, so alone and desolate. Poor Eleanor, how frightened she must have been.

When we reflect on what we are doing in our everyday life, we are always ashamed of ourselves.

In a flurry of belatedness and apology, I kissed her. Her beauty seemed to me as tragic as the flowers that no one bothered even to cut or put in a vase: nature's superfluity. "In this heat," she observed, "champagne is so much more refreshing than tea." She was on her best behavior. It was a pleasure to be in France again—a light-of-love country which, making no claims on her esteem, was the more likeable and refreshing. New York on the other hand is in a constant state of mutation. There all the time without you: and ever shall be, world without end.

She was silent for a while, inhaling, exhaling, wrapping herself in a veil of smoke. Her unassailable assumption of conquest. She often refers to herself as "the poor man's Kitty Carlisle Hart." But her beauty was the fragile kind that would fade or turn gaunt with age, and marred by lines around her mouth and faint shadows under her eyes.

Her feelings came down to me now in just dwindlements of the original. She stressed her words in unusual places, making them interesting and quite new-sounding. Naturally she is very nervous. "David," she said, "is only doing with you what he does with me."

Brava! She stood there, her fingers clenched, and the awful look of malevolence gathered and deepened on her face. I am but a man, and she was more than a woman.

In any case, I was now interested only in reading and writing and anonymous sex.

Anxiety like a distant ship, very far off. Anxiety being the fundamental mood of existence, as somebody once said, or unquestionably should have. I expected sympathy, if only feigned; after all, my life was about to change, and not for the better.

౮ 5 ౷

The weather had begun behaving in the most peculiar fashion. It was hot, yet with a sweet languor about it all.

I spent that morning in a mood of taut neutrality. I was lying on the back verandah trying to get interested in one of those contemporary overintrospective novels which I knew I ought to read but didn't really want to. I read it but couldn't understand it. The only fact one could deduce from it about the author is that he liked opera. I like to read novels in which the heroine has a costume rustling discreetly over her breasts, or discreet breasts rustling under her costume; in any case there must be a costume, some breasts, some rustling, and, over all, discretion.

There is no language without deceit.

Above me, in the intense blue of the summer sky, some faint brown shreds of cloud whirled into nothingness. Here we are, alone again. Take a few breaths.

I felt naked in a strange world.

So I enter upon a new and decisive phase in my life. In many respects, this is a grim prospect. What stumps me about myself is how—even now, midway through a season of trying to prick up my powers of attention—how oblivious I am. Everything was becoming confused. I kept having dreams of such terrible things happening. Why do we dream at all?

I used to be at peace with myself. But gay men—like straight women—always feel they're too old.

We always worry about the wrong things, don't we?

I am almost inclined to give up all my efforts.

The razor-sharp edges of companionship and love.

৪ 6 ৫

My decision to change my life was not all that easy to act upon. I lacked both genius and talent. I am forty years old. Beneath everything else I smelled (or rather heard) the melancholy of an old, waterlogged industrial building, a sound as virile but at the same time as sexless as a Russian basso descending liturgically from low G to F to E, on and on down on narrow steps below the stave into a resonant deep C. The place was scrubbed daily, but you could never eliminate the smell. The problem is much more serious than that. I opened the window, and the air entered in a single gust, as though it had been waiting for admission.

Generally, even then, I was lonely. A lost soul is one lost in the size and complexity of life. That's me.

The psychological feeling of dependence seems to be on the increase.

I dropped David a hint of what was going on. "Did you know that I have a son?"

Several times he made as though to speak, but sighed instead.

David extended his hand. "I'm so sorry," he said impulsively; "but you *are* among friends here, you know."

The things one tardily becomes aware of.

"I am glad you've come," he said, kissing me absently,

"because you, unlike many others I could name, occasionally understand what I am talking about."

The irony of this observation never seemed to occur to him.

"How are you getting on with your shrink?" he asked, somewhat irritated. He does not know that the passage from irritated love to black anger is short and swift, while the passage from anger to love is long, slow, and difficult.

"I am the father of an illegitimate son."

There was a short, smiling silence. But soon this spirit of confidence was followed by a feeling of blank pessimism. What, if anything, does he still want? What was the meaning of it all? Who will speak—who will fill the silence with whatever comes to mind?—and by so doing declare himself the loser, the bitch; the one willing to devise some conversation gambit so that everything can be okay.

"Which cathedral do you like best?" I asked in a strangled voice, trying hard to be natural.

A moan burst from David's lips. He was handsome and bold and pleasant, off-hand and gay and kind. His broad shoulders made him come off as a big man, though when he turned sideways his waist was breathtakingly slender. "But you have to settle in to looking at these things. You are too intellectual, my dear. It's too serious a question to decide at this late hour."

Amused, I nodded in agreement.

"I may be back late tonight," he said.

We will see. "Fortunately, I know you don't mean that."

"I'm interested in a lot of things," he bragged.

"Ah."

His leisure hours were often drunkenly aimless. There is, of course, in some young men, a certain drive to try to seduce everybody. He was young; he was boyish; he did but as nature bade him. And so on. He was a poet himself.

Take care of yourself, I love you so desperately. Do you love me?

ℬ 7 ℭ

The cuckoo came out of its clock, surveyed the scene and retreated, having remarked on the half hour. It was a dark rainy evening and there was no sound in the house. Summer was a hot blanket we got under.

Inwardness, calm, solitude make us less miserable.

No, that's too easy.

Silence.

At one point I snuck a glance at Joe. I must photograph those well-lashed eyes. Little ineffectual unquenchable flames! It was the expression of his face as a whole, however, that was disquieting. He was looking at the corn-cob which, because I like it, I had lying on my window ledge. He is not yet fully awake but in a state between sleep and waking in which everything appears unreally real. Solitude had acted on his brain like a narcotic, first exciting and stimulating him, then inducing a languor haunted by vague reveries, vitiating his plans, nullifying his intentions, leading a whole cavalcade of dreams to which he passively submitted, without even trying to get away. At school, he manifested a vindictiveness of disposition which made him feared and disliked. The other children noticed something dandified and 'Parisian' in him, although he had been raised exactly as they were. In the meantime he had become the most sharp-witted fool around. There was an air of desperation and possible violence around him like a rank perfume. He's a beautiful child, a little solemn sometimes, which I guess is allowable under the circumstances. It hurts to be this pure.

I have often wondered what it would have been like to have been born into a family that read books or liked any of the arts.

I admit I feel ill at ease with a great deal of literature. (In Wilde's phrase: "A truth in art is that whose contradiction is also true.")

Similarly, I sometimes wonder what life would have been like had I grown up in a world where being gay was accepted and understood.

We can only try day by day to seem to be someone else.

ೞ 8 ೞ

By Thanksgiving, Joe was back for a visit, sharing my room in the absence of my roommate. He stayed at home for several days feeling desolate and listening to a recording of countertenor David Daniels singing Handel arias. He asked me what I thought Eternity was like, and all I could offer was a guess—an Olivia de Havilland movie on television. "Even if there were rebirth," I said, "if you remember nothing of your previous existence, it's the same as turning into nothing, isn't it? I don't want the responsibility. I am like everyone else."

We're going to die.

Salvation lies in paying full attention to nature.

"Can't you smell something?" he asked. "What is it?" he asked as he turned on the dishwasher. I suddenly thought he was probably a homo. He was the sort of boy that becomes a clown and a lout as soon as he is not understood, or feels himself held cheap; and, again, is adorable at the first touch of warmth. What had been asleep in him was now awake. It was like the hum of countless children's voices—but yet not a hum, the echo rather of voices singing at an infinite distance—blended by sheer impossibility into one high but resonant sound that vibrated on the ear as if it were trying to penetrate beyond mere hearing.

"Yes, yes, I know. I feel in you a terrible exasperation. You must have guessed by now that I'm in love. You're not angry, are you, Joe?"

"No," said Joe tartly, "I'm not."

I want his life still to be his, mine to be mine.

"I think that you have just learned something new about yourself. Anyway, you'll get over it."

"Will you?" said Joe eagerly. "What is that you're wearing?" he asks. "Men are such perverts."

Score one for undeluded youth.

The world was swamped in tears. The nature of humanity is contradictory: man is a worm and at the same time divine; a slave and at the same time a ruler.

But in all, I'm satisfied to be here for the time being, I like the quiet—the city would flatten me. I get bored in the city. This is the theory anyway. To me there is nothing better than a damp, grey day, and a damp, grey mist, and greyness all about me, and freedom to become a part of it. In the course of that peculiar malady which ravages effete, enfeebled races, the crises are succeeded by sudden intervals of calm. But the city meant excitement and passion, the lure of the forbidden, the delights of sophisticated naughtiness.

"We are both orphans now," I said, after he'd come to my room and sat by me on the bed in the semi-dark. He was no longer just a runaway scamp but, at least in his mother's eyes, a juvenile delinquent. "You're probably wondering why I've brought this up." He begins to sob.

Joe looked at me with a quivering lip, and fairly put his sleeve before his eyes. Every heartstring is plucked. It would be an exaggeration to say that children see adults as they really are, but, like servants, they see them at moments when they are not concerned with making a favorable impression. It took him nearly five minutes to recover. The eloquence of Joe's arm surpassed the most impassioned language; and so did that of his lips—yet he said nothing, either. The silence speaks the scene.

Like a big dog nuzzling at his master, he crouched and pushed his head against my shoulder and sat down beside me with his knees drawn up, apparently intending to sleep that way. He knew I loved him.

Thank God for your daddy, boy. You can count on me.

Everybody knows you need young blood in your house.

"I'm the man in the house now," he used to say to his mother with joy. He knocked at the master bedroom door. "I am!" said Joe, in a very decided manner.

But many questions remained to be considered on other fronts.

Either way, I call the shots around here.

☙ 9 ❧

David watched my preparations with distasteful levity, but anon made a noble amend by abruptly offering me his foot as if he had no longer use for it, and I knew by intuition that he expected me to take off his boots. "You hear what your father says, Joe? We must be patient, Joe, and bear with the old folks' foibles. You're so reluctant to show any enthusiasm about anything, or even allow it in other people. Am I upsetting you?" He looked over for some confirmation, but Joe was busy with the remote. "Oh, you'll see," said David. Here he poured himself out another glass of wine.

Joe could only repeat his former eloquence, but it was very much to the purpose. "You're useless," he says. He told him only that he was relying on his loyalty and hatred. "It's not my way to sacrifice my existence to sentimentality. Don't we all discover at some stage or another that there are some things we'll never get any better at, even though we have no idea why and hardly ever notice it when it happens, even though we may have enjoyed these things and might not have been lagging behind last time we checked? We identify with an ideal image, only to be plagued by a nagging sense of failing to live up to the ideal."

David gave a little gulp; not only were these beautiful words, but they meant something... He crawled back to bed, exhausted now. Words, words, words. Every morning, he woke up in the firmly locked cell of a new age-old day. He looked forward to the night.

Well, never mind him.

We observe our children, and in observing them imagine that we have somehow shaped them.

๛ 10 ๛

Back in the capital the revels continued. Even the self-deprecating Eleanor admitted that her eyes were her best feature. We spent the evening and that whole night together. We discovered (very late at night such a discovery is inevitable) that there is something monstrous about mirrors. Eleanor gave a little laugh. She was wearing a French perfume so dark it was almost carbolic, and her primrose shirt was dirty. It was that windless hour of dawn when madness wakes and strange plants open to the light and the moth flies forth silently. I viewed her—as I did all women, perhaps—as a lady stranded in circumstances beyond her control. She flung herself on the sofa, the bed, the floor. "What a city this is! Paris is the aphrodisiac of cities—even tops Rome. When I look at the city of Paris I long to wrap my legs around it." This is in fact what happened. "Is it a dream?" she says. "Do you know any love poems?"

As if.

I rose from my knees. I've had it with adventures, I said in a tiny little voice. Let them think we are unhappy and vicious, if they want, for the time being. But in France?

This is real life. Swarms of crows were circling round it.

The fact is that when the period in which a man of talent is condemned to live is dull and stupid, the artist is haunted, perhaps unknown to himself, by a nostalgic yearning for another age. To me it is a prison.

"Well," she says, "what's it gonna be?" She moved in for another kiss. She was as drunk as she was beautiful. She was bizarre, a kind of human oxymoron.

"No means no this time." Perhaps you can only really love a virgin—a virgin in body and mind—a delicate bud which has not yet been caressed by any zephyr, a bud whose unseen breast has not received the raindrop or the pearl of the dew, a chaste flower which unfurls its white robe only for you, a beautiful lily gilded only by your sun, swayed by your breath and watered by your hand.

"If you're hungry, it's natural to think always of food." She went back to the kitchen, where she forgot what she had intended to do next, and sat down in a chair by the kitchen table. Her thoughts were in themselves a form of locomotion. She is inexhaustibly obliging, and enters perfectly into all my whims, however bizarre they may be. And though there was no one to admire her, she was quite content to admire herself—indeed, a great part of her high spirits and good-humour sprang from her solitary and unprotected state. Her eyes sparkled brilliantly and wrathfully; one of her stockings had slipped down. What can I do? she thought. She did not like to stay at home.

I understand. A woman whom a man betrays for another man knows that all is lost. I had been, as it were, caught in the act.

To poeticize oneself into a girl is an art, to poeticize oneself out of her a masterpiece. It is something to do with the gaze, of course, but there is more to it than that.

She turned, and sprang towards me like a tigress. "What have you ever known about women?" she demanded with some petulance. She repeated all the foulest and most humiliating insults that men and women had ever thrown at her. For if there was one thing that she preferred to a complete success, it was a real fiasco.

Imagine what that does to my writing: how it deforms my idiom and inhibits my voice. "You think of everything," I said. She was really beginning to get on my nerves with her whining. I am nonviolent. Luckily, the industrial-strength earplugs I had purchased in Tucson were holding up well against the onslaught. It's still too early to make concessions. "I wish I knew what you were talking about," I said plaintively. The indifference in my voice surprised me. What makes us think, or why would we want to think, that the more we know about people the more we will like them?

The evening ended on a sour note.

The great revolutions are always metaphysical.

If, as John Lennon said, life is what happens to you when you are doing something else, then so, perhaps, is happiness.

ೞ 11 ೞ

Now that the nights were so hot I went to bed late. At night this road is unlit, desolate, anonymous; it exists not on earth but as a path among clouds, miles from everywhere; an infinity separates it from the sleepers who snore in the small indistinguishable houses on either of its sides. Cars were rare and there were stars at night. The black cattle were grazing just beyond the fence; and the chains around the necks of the aristocrats among them tinkled in the darkness. Night music. Most of the houses on the back roads were inhabited by childless couples or old bachelors or widows living alone. But the people who thrive here—and there aren't many of them—are an interesting species.

The high cold empty gloomy rooms liberated me and I went from room to room singing. 2:00 – 5:00 every day I shall set aside for writing and study outside in the sun, and whatever time in the evenings I can manage—I shall be quiet, courteous, and disinvolved!

The pen was cool to the touch. I wrote about women, hatefully, cruelly, I wrote about homosexuals and children lost in derelict railway stations. I could go on forever if I could. Every book is in a sense autobiographical. How deep-seated a habit it is: a lifetime of self-revelation, self-anatomization. Like an earnest woman in pregnancy, I have observed beautiful forms and colours, and listened carefully to harmonious sound, in the hope that such experiences might somehow become incorporate in me and pleasantly affect my issue. It is up to us to determine the meaning our life stories have. These are the much-celebrated Sebald's abiding questions. They lived und laughed ant loved end left. What a difference there is between one book and another!

I am forever getting advice from well-meaning friends—and knowledgeable professional advisers—to "go commercial." Silly seasons always are with us. Tinkering over sentences at my computer, I believed, really and truly, that a great cyclotron of art was at hand.

Lately, my sexual life has become very pure. Revenge fucking may not be the sweetest sex, nor the most satisfying, but it's the most urgent. I felt excellent. Nonetheless my condition of feeling quite guilty continued for the longest time. Loners can be morbidly sensitive to this sort of thing.

It was all too good to be true.

Unending flights of screeching birds, which skimmed low over the water, from afar resembled drifting islands.

Other people see us in ways that we cannot anticipate; we cannot know ourselves because we cannot be everyone else in relation to ourselves; and so on.

I entered silently, sat beside the sleeping boy for a moment, then wandered about the other room. Then I stood in front of the mirror and stayed like that for so long that my reflection became a stranger and looked absurd. After that it was necessary to hold sadness at bay with a brandy, though not successfully.

Writers are a scourge to those they cohabit with. Our ears, our minds, our mouths, are stuffed with personalities. The better you try to be, the bigger mess you make. Yet I could not, would not, dismiss my beloved boy.

I am beginning to catch sight of what I might call the "deep-lying" subject of my book. I have always, all of my life, been looking for help from a man. And this must be where my mistake is.

My mother's femaleness was absolute, ancient, and there was a peculiar, helpless assertiveness about it. My mother was a faded old lady, sort of like the Queen of England. This was her only form of self-defense. And walking in vain, suddenly she would sit down on one of the circus chairs that stood by the long window overlooking the garden, bend forward, putting her hands between her legs, and begin to cry, "Oh, God! Oh, God! Oh, God!" repeated so often that it had the effect of all words spoken in vain. For nothing could stop my mother when she reentered the past and plunged back into her disastrous childhood. The dizziness and queer sensations that sometimes followed she took to be a proof of how much good it was doing her. Women baffled me, my mother in particular.

I was born between two miscarriages. It was an ill wind that blew nobody good. It was 1968. A sordid sexual event had occurred at some point.

From the beginning I sense that something is wrong. It's something almost imperceptible. Grown-ups tried to sweeten the pill, but there was no hiding it, children were the most oppressed creatures on earth. I was a bastard child, I had no right to the social order.

My mother was completely out of my control; she was two women, and which of them would be seated on the porch when I got home from school I never knew beforehand. Days and nights were like verses of an infinitely harmonious dark song to us. After I had run away from school, no one knew what to do with me. I knew that I had a facility with words and a power of facing unpleasant facts, and I felt that this created a sort of private world in which I could get my own back from my failure in everyday life. I became a voracious reader; I was ambitious for an intellectual life I imagined belonging only to towers, gray cities, winter—to monks in cold cells, poets in scarves, women in furs, Edmund Wilson. Land of noble ideas. New York City rose out of the sea looking like nothing on earth. New York seemed like a mirage to me. Meanwhile, the possibility of the lone genius remained. Thank you, Proust. I was glad that I was going to be alone.

Then the amazing thing happened. My mother wanted me to be a homosexual. "My dear," she cried, "I'm going to give you this dress as soon as I'm through with it." My childhood was not, however, quite the gay whirl that one might imagine from the above statement. My mother has always been a heavy drinker. My father went crazy and became a cocaine fiend. Though long dead, he is very much alive in my dream.

Insanity, of course, runs in families; and it was, perhaps, too much to expect me to escape it.

We find our true nature writ small but clear in our childhood lives.

"I didn't," said Joe, "until to-night. My experience of life is that it's very fragmented."

Perhaps the least cheering statement ever made on the subject of art is that life imitates it. Yet any distinction between literature and life is misleading.

⟶ 12 ⟵

David woke next morning very early, with a sense of immense interest in things in general. He changed some of his pet habits—that of spending Sunday morning at the Turkish baths for instance. At all events, it was in the autumn that he resolved to become the greatest writer of all time. There were so many different moods and impressions that he wished to express in verse. He regarded himself as working in a state of aesthetic revolution, even against himself: "Many times I've put myself up against the wall and shot myself." He had many literary friends. It was a pity his name was not more Irish-looking. He tried to weigh his soul to see if it was a poet's soul. For the moment his most basic decision was in favor of art's precedence over every other human activity.

He felt that he loved his wife sincerely, tenderly—as much in fact as he was capable of loving a human being; and he was perfectly frank with her in everything except that secret foolish craving, that dream, that lust burning a hole in his life. He had a life apart from her—his sexual life. The idea of secrecy is the last refuge of romance. I am sure they are very good friends. Which made it particularly ticklish. Mind you, he was still the tenderest of husbands, in fact, more than tender, a perfect angel. His wife was well satisfied. But nobody came. Obscurely, each thought—or fondly hoped— the other was sliding into musty celibacy. She noticed that the people whom he passed looked back after him; but he went straight forward, lifting above them a face like a February sky. At such moments he was horrified by a sudden awareness of his own insufficiency and a profound sense of failure. It's corny, it's sentimental, he doesn't talk to people about it, but it feels at certain times—now, for instance—like his most essential aspect: his conviction, in the face of all evidence to the contrary, that some terrible, blinding beauty is about to descend and, like the wrath of God, suck it all away, orphan us, deliver us, leave us wondering how exactly we're going to start it all over again. "I suppose I am just a half-man," he used to say bitterly. The metaphor wasn't so far off the mark.

I was still not entirely happy with the sleeping arrangements. But one has to admit that if there is one domain in which, in discourse, deception has some chance of success, it is certainly love that provides its model. There are moments when the force of marriage—not love but marriage—is greater than the force of the individuals who must endure it. It was all quite dazzling. Moral: slack beds make slick battlefields.

I rubbed his shoulders and arms and back and buttocks and legs and feet and buttocks and shoulders and buttocks. The poor man, the malleable, pitiable, wretched man. Still, he has all the nerves in the usual places. I didn't like him, but at that moment I wanted to fuck him more than I'd ever wanted to do anything in my life. I told him I was writing a comedy.

A dreadful silence overcharged with bathos followed.

❧ 13 ☙

By late September Joe was back in New York, depressed. My son lived a life of laziness and luxury. But he came home lonely, penniless and discouraged. To travel without a maid was not possible. One day while talking about his mother he made an interesting Freudian slip and instead of my mother said, my money.

He lay half the morning behind his eyelids, a prey to visions of electric flowers flickering with girls' faces, of such banality he grew ashamed. We've been discussing the soul. He slouched down opposite me, ordered a Coke, pushed the glasses up on to his lovely head of blond hair and quizzically cocked his sun-kindled features. "When I try to do arithmetic clouds come down upon me like they do in Tannhauser." The slight asymmetry of the center dip in the cupid's bow of his upper lip is one of those intriguing flaws in an otherwise perfect face that makes the viewer catch his breath. I liked being with him as I like being with swift animals who are motionless when at rest. Those who meet him become calm and purified.

"This," I said to him, "is the happiest moment of my life." Believe it or not, I am reasonably happy.

"Who, slow down," said Joe. "Do you really mean that?" All his life Joe had dreamed of an all-consuming love that would go on forever. I exaggerate, of course. He never gave much thought to questions of the future. That would be too bourgeois. But in general, as Joe put it, "I hate being in any situation that is over with." He waggled a portentous eyebrow. "When one is frightened of the truth (as I am now) then it is never the whole truth that one has an inkling of." He was so lonely, he often sat on the steps in someone else's house and thought he was going to die of misery. The sadness of sophistication has come to the boy. He remembered his dreams and transcribed some of them into a copybook. In this he would write till midnight chimed and long after. "Thank you for the dream book. Where did you get that thing?" The book was a present. Joe had been doing a lot of art work, most of it hallucinatory. It is all strangely fantastic, phantasmagoric. I could not help thinking of the scene in which poor Gregor Samsa, his little legs trembling, climbs the armchair and looks out of his room, no longer remembering (so Kafka's narrative goes) the sense of liberation that gazing out of the window had formerly given him.

The price he exacted for submitting himself to so much culture was the frequent excursions that we made together into the world of popular entertainment. It seemed to amuse him, so I complied with his odd request. I am a white American male who listened to nothing but classical music until the age of twenty. I felt myself sliding deliciously downwards into a miasma of kindliness. That is how everything works, pluses and minuses. Silence, he said, was of all things the most oppressive to his nerves.

We take long walks among the flying leaves and ponder turnings taken by our lives. Sunshine, a bird with a special, rather literary song, country noises (a motor), solitude, peace, no aggression. Forced to make do, we do rather well.

You never stop learning, that's what's great about life. Apart from that, I really can't think of anything. To all appearances it looks like calm, like I'm unflappable. Or maybe not.

It was that dim grey hour when things are just creeping out of darkness, when everything is colourless and clear cut, and yet unreal. The other houses on the street, conscious of decent lives within them, gazed at one another with brown imperturbable faces. Joe said, "I'm confident I can teach myself everything I want to know by reading books and seeking out the knowledge that interests me." Then he was silent for a long time, shuddering and sighing like an animal. He wanted to be a veterinarian. He believed that animals, too, have souls and that man is an intermediate link in the chain of beings connecting the world of animals and the world of pure spirits. "All you've got to do is simply learn to resist yourself. In other words, there are all sorts of things that happen that make us…that let us make one choice rather than another, hmm? You have to tell a story! I will not be silent anymore. Humility is a quality for which I have only a limited admiration. Our twentieth century has been almost one long holocaust of world wars and local genocidal conflicts, with the largest losses of life being caused by huge bureaucratic governments systematically exterminating their own subjects. The aim of life, Freud says, is death, is the return of the organic to the inorganic, supposedly our earlier state of being. One last point. The future has not yet produced anything to be happy about. Everyone today will agree that the world we have fabricated during the last two hundred years is hideous compared with any fabricated in earlier times."

44.

What a strange mind! He dismissed bourgeois society as a mechanism lacking the poetic element, an agglomeration of individuals motivated by self-interest and not held together by any moral bonds. Among the strongest impulses of his imagination was an urge to find parallels and connections between events that occur on a local, human scale and events that occur on the vastly larger scale of history, evolution, and cosmology.

Everywhere, between the houses, those old and dingy houses, whose windows would catch the sunrise with untold splendor, showed plots of garden, like snatches of old song. "The main thing," Joe says, "oh yeah, the mainest thing . . . is, when you fall, fall in the direction of your work."

I was stirred by these ideas. Fortunately, I am not a hysterical person. "Well, yeah," I philosophized. "You know what you should be doing, you know what is right, but that is not what you do." If you care to put it that way, you can say it is a simple story.

"I don't," said Joe. "Who is your favorite writer?"

"Karl Ove Knausgaard," I said.

Towards dark he went out.

I had been rescued from my solitude; I had been given another chance; and I had high hopes of a future that would cancel out the past. I of all people. Loveless, landless, wifeless. Since this sensation was utterly unfamiliar and not at all unpleasant I decided that, if experienced again, I

45.

would refer to it as contentment. I Google it. How quickly the mind swivels in response to what it learns.

I found myself in the same grey light and tumult I have already described.

All I could hear was the wind sweeping in from the country and buffeting the window; and in between, when the sound subsided, there was the never entirely ceasing murmur in my own ears. That's the ego.

Convinced life is meaningless, I lack the courage of my conviction.

ꙮ 14 ꙮ

An ambulance hurries to a home on a hilltop. The crimes sparkle in the moonlight.

If only I could commit a crime, and be done with it. My intentions are better than anything else about me. So much for "naturalness." In this sense, we are all artists, or death-artists.

"I'll teach you a thing or two, you little prick!" That's a pledge from the very bottom of my heart.

David laughed gleefully. He would love that, he said, better than anything in this world; and his voice, as he led me monotonously through the mystery, grew almost affectionate and seemed to plead with me that I should understand him. "Such as ...?" That indeed is the question. "There is happiness in doubting, I wonder why." Tilting his head back, he slowly released an enormous quantity of smoke from his mouth and drew it up through his nostrils. "Please, do not be evasive! We all live in a chattering crowd, each of us waiting for a chance to be heard. Do you know any compliments?"

"Nothing is got for nothing," I said. The writer does not 'wrest' speech from silence, as we are told in pious literary hagiographies, but inversely, and how much more arduously, more cruelly and less gloriously, detaches a secondary language from the slime of primary languages afforded him by the world, history, his existence, in short by an intelligibility which pre-exists him, for he comes into a world full of language, and there is no reality not already classified by men: to be born is nothing but to find this code ready-made and to be obliged to accommodate oneself to it. Thus every writer's motto reads: mad I cannot be, sane I do not deign to be, neurotic I am. I'd far rather leave a thought behind me than a child. After all, it has taken several degrees of contusion to create a jaundice as pervasive as mine. I was a very, very bad kid. Punish me, please."

"You are quite Voltairean!" he murmured. "Things can always get worse."

"Ah."

Longing for sweeter grass, he wanders away. "I don't care for children."

Very ingenious, one feels, but how much better not to have said it! And since, on occasion, he quotes Levinas, people take him for a great mind.

A moment later the engine roared and the tires squealed out of the driveway.

When I was left alone in his house, looking around the library, which was, in some mysterious way, the incarnation both of his absence and his presence, I asked his spirit (it was, of course, a rhetorical question) why things had turned out as they had for us. There was no denying it was interesting, but would it be enough to sustain a long-term relationship? It was fascinating, it was empty and spectacular, but after a few days it also got a bit boring. I work better alone. I forbade myself to go on brooding about it.

Leafing through a pile of books, I have been wondering if there has ever been in America a novelist with a point of view toward the taking and giving of pleasure even vaguely resembling Colette's, an American writer, man or woman, stirred as deeply as she is by scent and warmth and color, someone as sympathetic to the range of the body's urgings, as attuned to the world's every sensuous offering, a connoisseur of the finest gradations of amorous feeling, who is nonetheless immune to fanaticism of any sort, except, as with Colette, a fanatical devotion to the self's honorable survival.

ೞ 15 ಔ

Eleanor "sprang from a noble race."

"If you want to call it that," she said. "I'm always kind to people who have good Louis Quatorze. No one's supposed to know about that," she said, more resignedly than annoyed. I found it all repellent and queasy-making.

As a child she was lonely and shy in public, with a "desperate inner life." Once she thought she heard voices and stopped, only to hear nothing at all. At this point a wonderful piece of luck came her way. Flowering puberty. A great deal of what we value in civilized life depends upon it.

There were stormy scenes at home, sobs, moans, hysterics. And then, who knows how or why, the situation gradually improved. The struggle, if there were one, need not be described.

Traits that we all recognize in ourselves are, in her case, blown up into intense inner (and sometimes public) dramas. She was under the spell of that timorous curiosity which leads women to seek out dangerous emotions, to go see chained tigers, to look at boa constrictors, frightening themselves because they are separated from them only by weak fences.

Little is known about her mother—there were no exciting stories about her—who died when Eleanor was only eight years old. Eleanor took no notice, as if regarding such an incident as too trivial to heed. "To wrestle with a bad feeling only pins our attention on it, and keeps it still fastened in the mind: whereas, if we act as if from some better feeling, the old bad feeling soon folds its tent like an Arab, and silently steals away." The paradox is not confined to poetry.

She stood in the darkness leaning against the wall and watched Greta Garbo. Beside her was a Jewish boy, a hump-back, with a face that hunger had sharpened into a painful beauty. He smiled wistfully and touched her pretty hair and said, "You're gorgeous, you know," and went back to his room for the night. Eleanor loved the evening entertainment.

Everything lay beneath a peculiar shimmer that made all it touched smaller and more delicate; she felt a bit dizzy and sat down.

On such unproductive occasions I don't linger very long.

ༀ 16 ༃

I am sitting in my room, looking at the houses and gardens across the street, while all kinds of thoughts pass through my head. Scared of the trap of being less desired than I myself desire, the trap that is called being in love.

Better take two of those blue pills tonight.

The object in your hands is not a novel. Novels seem like desperate attempts at control, and poems like attempts at grandeur. The novel is a monumental waste of time.

The worse your art is, the American poet John Ashbery once remarked, the easier it is to talk about it. Originality is therefore the price which must be paid for the hope of being welcomed (and not merely understood) by your reader.

Miracles happen every day. Each is in a different style.

Introspection, however, is not to be enforced. Depression comes when, in the depths of despair, I cannot manage to save myself by my attachment to writing.

ಙ 17 ಚಿ

David gave a great sigh. "But where are you going, Eleanor?" At first, he was so overwhelmed by her beauty, her charm, and her powerful personality that he could scarcely speak. Suddenly their eyes met, and she smiled to him—a rare, intimate smile, beautiful with brightness and love. Now that this handsome young man was proving himself a reality she found herself vaguely trembling; she was deeply excited.

Please, David, she pleaded, you mustn't feel so badly. We only want to make you happy, to make you finally you, David dear.

Now he's really in trouble.

The deeper you go, as a writer, into the minds of your characters—the more detailed and refined your registration of their thoughts, feelings, sensations, memories, scruples— the slower the narrative tempo becomes, and the less action there is.

I was in the kitchen fixing iced concoctions. I will not let any gloomy moralizing intrude upon us here to-night.

I remain a while feeling deeply, or at least trying to feel deeply.

I returned to David, and asked him in a low voice whether he would give me a kiss.

"Oh, don't be tedious," said David. For now was no time for romance or enthusiasm. As soon as the conversation reached a certain level he would murmur: "Oh, no dreams and utopias, please!" The sense of love stirred in him, the love one always feels for what one has lost, whether a child, a woman, or even pain. But instead of being down in the mouth with fear, he felt elated by it, living, as he did, in a deep, violent and finally organic belief in his lucky star. His life has been an attempt to realize the task of living poetically. Poor, ridiculous young man. "He has a lovely smile," my mother liked to say. And David did some adorable things.

Everybody is feeling a little more cheerful about everything to-day even though it is a dark and gloomy day.

They danced at arm's length, their teeth bared in hostility. They attacked one another with obscure allusions and had a silly quarrel. "Do you think," he said to her, "that I might come and live with you in your house?"

When it was quiet, she turned towards him with a guilty laugh. She hadn't said, "Oh, yes, darling!" but it was understood.

"What the hell are you laughin' at?" he asked.

"Do not talk nonsense," said Eleanor, in a low tone. What if, for some one of the subtler reasons that would tell with both of them, they should tire of each other, misunderstand or irritate each other? She spoke amiably, yet with the least hint of dismissal in her voice. "Do you know how many men I've slept with the last two months?" Somehow she managed to look sleek and disheveled at the same time. It left her feeling slightly upset and annoyed, first with him and then with herself.

He listened carefully, as always, putting in an appropriate word or two. "In future we'll do our best to spare Mademoiselle's nerves." The night was full of an evil she didn't seem aware of, and he had failed to exorcize.

They were young and seemed to be in a bad mood, but at the time I felt they had sprung from a dream in which good and bad moods were no more than metaphysical accidents. One of the defects of my character is that I can never grow used to the plainness of people; however sweet a disposition a friend of mine may have, years of intimacy can never reconcile me to his bad teeth or lopsided nose: on the other hand I never cease to delight in his comeliness and after twenty years of familiarity I am still able to take pleasure in a well-shaped brow or the delicate line of a cheekbone.

She spoke of his many manly virtues, and extolled the human qualities which made him a helper of the weak and frail, because he himself was weak and frail. Kindness personified; very capable; dapper through and through; antique-loving. "The trouble is, my dear, that he has not yet found the right woman." She really knows how to exasperate me.

They agreed on all points, and aroused each other to a ridiculous pitch of enthusiasm over nothing in particular. "And now you are going to have a change," said Eleanor, with a condoning smile and a sense of relief, as solemn spirits on seriously joyful occasions affected her as they did most people. One of the three silver rings she wears is taloned, like an obscure torture implement.

"Just like a mother," he said. She is nothing but sexuality; she is sexuality itself. He withdraws again, nibbles her ear, moves to her neck and traces, with his tongue, the exposed part of her chest.

Then there was silence; and a cow coughed; and that led her to say how odd it was, as a child, she had never feared cows, only horses. "That's why I always like Englishmen."

"Amen," sang David fervently, looking as if he had just come down from an Italian picture of singing angels. Not knowing what to say, he accented his awkwardness, playing the inoffensive fool.

He hadn't meant to live like this or among these third-rate people.

This scene was not positively comical; however, it was imbued with a strangeness, or if you like a naturalness, the beauty of which continued to grow. The Beautiful is always strange.

"You seem a sufficiently intelligent young man. You look good enough to eat. Don't insult me, David, please. Throw me down and beat me, you dirty little coward! Do you prefer that?"

He refused, but not without a struggle. "It's not out of laziness," he replied very seriously, "but to maintain my dignity."

His contempt of Nietzsche, whom she adored, was intolerable. They thrill him, these little demonstrations of womanly certainty.

She was so trapped and entranced by his passion for her that it seemed to her now as though she might care for him as much as he wished. "But at the same time I've been threatening for months to give up *la vie sexuelle*—and maybe this is the time to do it." These are the falsifications that survival can require of us. "I'm perfectly willing to take my chances," she said.

"I wouldn't be caught dead in them," he said.

"It's true I'm not clever enough to bake banana bread and carrot bread and raise my own bean sprouts and 'audit' seminars and 'head up' committees to outlaw war for all time, but people still look at me, David, wherever I go."

O dear, o dear, o dear. Colette had it right. Thus women are naturally, inescapably, untruthful.

Returning to the door of the drawing-room, where there were more people now and everything seemed to be moving in a sort of luminous haze, David stood there watching the dancing, half shutting his eyes in order to see better, and breathing in the languorous scent of the women, which filled the room like a vast, ubiquitous kiss. He kicked the door shut behind him, then stood in the middle of the room, his face screwed up with rage. "What did I tell you?" he started screaming.

"Well, what a lot of smoke without any flame!" said Eleanor, not looking into anyone's face. She herself was something of a princess turned into a swine-girl in her own imagination. "Young people are so sad!" she said. "We are so spiritual."

And his dark, liquid, nervous eyes, looking anywhere but at her. "Her voice is full of money," he said suddenly.

She took it as a compliment. She came forward, very businesslike, her hat pushed forward like a greedy bird. "And you really don't despise me?" she asked, smiling through her tears, which was difficult, seeing there were no tears to smile through. The voice was so faint he could just barely hear it. This no longer seemed fun to us.

Once we have taken Evil into ourselves, it no longer insists that we believe in it.

Angry, and half in love with her, and tremendously sorry, I turned away. We have to read others as they have to read us, and where there is reading there is bound to be misreading, and doubt about which is which. Though I concealed my anger, I tried to make it clear that I was doing so. We love women in so far as they are strangers to us.

I went out into pale damaged daylight, twilight already falling. "You won't stay there long!" David exclaimed.

He spent the next few days chatting with Eleanor and trying (unsuccessfully) to make his way through Ivy Compton-

Burnett's *More Women Than Men.*

They need me, don't you think?

❧ 18 ❧

"What are you laughing at?" said David, raising his voice. He means to be rigorous, not hard; he himself is appalled by how he can sound.

"Why, David," said I, sitting up, "do you want to come into my bed?"

He'd spent half the day, if not all of it, drunk out of his wits. *The Magic Mountain* sits open but unread on his lap. He wished that he too could be carried away on waves of emotion. But it opens up the night to the risks of the dark side; these should not be underestimated. The wish always to be somewhere else, at least in one's mind.

He had a sad penchant for becoming enamoured of his wife's lovers. I gathered from David that this depressed her exceedingly. "Such missteps," he added as an aside, "are unavoidable ever since we ate of the fruit of the tree of knowledge."

I don't know what sort of a genre this is. A kind of epic without the heroic attitude.

He wailed loudly and choked on his tears. It was depressing as hell. "She loves me," he said, raising his tear-drenched face as though he must drive the unlikely statement home. Oh, incompetence! If you can unpack your heart with words, then what you express is already dead within you.

I sigh, depressed, and grind my teeth. "Yes," I said, "I can see that." I pulled myself back from politeness. The more I thought afterwards about what he said, the more uneasy it made me. If a man's reason succumbs to the pull of his senses he is lost. Love is an "impounding" of someone else's desirable beauty. Such an old story.

Times like this, I curse the human race.

I'm just trying to be a good father. This is not something that comes easily to me.

He dropped his bag and in a cold sweat sunk down, crouching behind a tall, thick tree, rigid and motionless with fear. "I'm sorry about the luggage," he said, "I know it's pretentious."

The supreme vice is shallowness. David himself had already begun to believe it.

He looked me straight in the eyes. I knew I looked very attractive. "I pretended she was you. But you see," he said, "I don't think two men can love each other . . . in that way." What an unnatural act—or was it? He was also very attractive. "The basis of character is will-power, and my will-power became absolutely subject to yours. The mind obeys the body. But maybe not. All day long I've been thinking of her. I had not believed it possible to give such pleasure, to satisfy such a variety of moods, to feel so demanded and so secure, to be loved by anyone so beautiful and to see that beauty enhanced by loving me. My private life has been dangerous from the beginning. We don't need to examine that. But think about it for a moment. One has to restrict oneself, that is a main condition of all enjoyment."

No thanks.

David talked in short bursts. "So I have considered gathering material for a book, entitled *Contribution to the Theory of the Kiss*, dedicated to all tender lovers. At least *I* have a style!" he concluded.

That is our ambition, that is our goal. But a style is only a start.

"To tell the truth, I'm afraid of you," he added, by way of explanation.

Oh, *pardon, madame!* "Do you expect me to believe that?"

It was too late to go anywhere I knew people. The street is full of humiliations to the proud. The fairies perched on a couple of windowsills. As long as we are not burned at the stake or locked up in asylums, we continue to flounder in the ghettoes of nightclubs, public restrooms and sidelong glances, as if that misery had become the habit of our happiness. Young people, especially young gay men, migrate to big cities for just this reason.

I wanted to do something spectacular to blot out the silly scene upstairs; and I could think of nothing. It was too late. In any modern city, a great deal of our energy has to be expended in *not* seeing, *not* hearing, *not* smelling. "All right, let's go to a hotel. The purpose is to keep you gay."

"I'd love to, but it's got to be quick." In the translucent darkness between the trees he moved with a tread more like hovering over a cushion of moss a foot thick. "I can't tell you anything until you sit down." His warm, masculine voice seemed to mesh beautifully with the mildness of the night. David's head dropped in a gesture of despondency. Added to this was an increasing sense of isolation.

"Why," I said, "do you think you've wasted your life?" I threw him a quick glance: he really did not understand what I was talking about, could not for the life of him see what I was getting at.

"I don't sleep well," he replied softly. "What are you writing?"

It was an idiotic conversation and on one level I couldn't believe we were actually having it. The intellectual attitude it is expressive of is one of disoriented agnosticism. I was astonished at how light and lighthearted this left me. "What do you think of this garden?" It's good at first to be out in the night, naked to the cold mechanics of the stars.

"Doesn't matter what I think," said David. He was lying on his back, staring at the flies that buzzed overhead. He had given up trying to find out if words generated feelings or merely serve them. He had never lingered among the pleasures of memory. It is not conscious knowledge, or fresh knowledge, but the knowledge one did not know that one knew, or but dimly knew, that bursts upon one, an access of strength; and it bursts from inside where it has been nurtured with every unconscious skill.

"I wasn't trying to insult you," I said. Nothing, however, could prevent his inner consciousness inflicting on him the punishment which ate into his spirit like rust, and which he could only alleviate by drinking. For "style" has been his disaster. "Well, what is it?"

I heard some squirting sounds I couldn't decipher.

"Listen," he said, "they're playing our song."

Opportunity sometimes knocks very softly.

Another long silence followed.

How the hell does one keep out of romanticism? We should strive to be neither happy nor unhappy, but serenely unconscious of ourselves.

But I am beginning now to fear that I must wait a lifetime.

✌ 19 ✍

Strange beds have rarely agreed with me, and after only a short spell of somewhat troubled slumber, I awoke an hour or so ago. A spot of insomnia is not without its uses for appreciating sleep, for projecting a certain light into that darkness. I was—and this admission pains me—I was terribly sexually frustrated and plagued by the most frenzied erotic fantasies, the majority of them completely impracticable, technically speaking (knowing next to nothing about sex and its usual positions since I'd devoted my entire libido to literature, I lacked basic physiological information, notably sensory-motor knowledge, and I imagined fantastic interlocking positions, unfeasible contortions, implausible spiraling, furious loop-the-loops, flips, entanglements, triple somersaults, and acrobatic stunts). Was love insane sex-hunger? I, too, wanted to make men leave their wives and run off with me. I know the type; most of my friends are case studies. I, too, wanted to escape the ennui of my petit-bourgeois world and embrace bohemia.

David sat quietly, surrounding a beer, still unhappy over the earlier conversation. "Anarchy," he said, "is out to upset everything, even the proper relationship of man and woman."

I made no reply, perhaps out of laziness, and, it seems to me, so as to be less alive. My mind drifts. Life in the temperate zone was full of fears and inhibitions, but in the tropics. . . .

It was too exhausting: it was too cruel. Yet the vulnerable young creature was, I believe, already half inside the trap I was setting for him; I could read in his eyes how he still craved to gorge on the praise and attention the inadequacies of his career had hitherto denied him; and although I could not afford to have him too alarmed, the course to which I had committed myself was irreversible and there was nothing for me now but to press home what I felt to be my advantage.

"I have no one in the world but you." I say that as much to comfort myself as to state something I think to be true. Life has but one true charm: the charm of gambling.

"I like men who have a future, and women who have a past," he answered. "There's a something to be said for wives," he added, folding his arms and crossing his outstretched legs. He said that he would do everything I wished. Tentatively, he added that it looked like his generation would be the first for whom AIDS was simply a chronic illness. Then he smiled, and in a new good-natured manner launched into a funny story about some friend of his, an opera singer who once, in the part of Lohengrin, being tight, failed to board the swan in time and waited hopefully for the next one.

He liked to say that genius is memory. In truth, however hard you try, you can never retrieve an experience in full. Behind our thoughts, true and false, there is always to be found a dark background, which we are only later able to bring into the light and express as a thought. He raised his glass, the way he used to when he was on a roll, so someone would get him a refill (usually me). I ignored this. "I must kiss you once more," he said. "One night," he said, "I'm going to—what are you stopping for?"

He was a fearful man. Sexy. His favorite instrument was the cello, and Béla Bartók his favorite composer. A local artist painted his portrait in bed, looking like a little kid with a child's illness—mumps of the soul, perhaps. Asleep, or perhaps sitting up writing love lyrics to his inamorata—inamoratus, that was more correct.

He picked up his little suitcase from the floor and went out.

The men I was not in love with have been more satisfactory in bed than the men I loved. That can hardly be unimportant. I wish I had a simple explanation—or, indeed, any kind of an explanation—to account for this rather unusual phenomenon (if I did, I'd patent it). As Gertrude Stein said, Life is funny that way.

ℬ 20 ℭ

You can imagine what it's like, when you open yourself like a book, and find misprints everywhere, one after another, misprints on every page! This is Eleanor's story. Her whole life is like that. Life-bloated, baffled, long-suffering hag. She was woebegone, and so dejected that in all seasons one saw around her the stiff rushes and pure puddles of a swamp. She has given self-love a bad name. When she walked up to the closed window and looked steeply down into the little back garden, she was overcome by a kind of vertigo. "The force of gravity," she remarked to the night; and suddenly the foolish words seemed to clinch her despair, shutting her up for ever in the residue of a life without joy, purpose or possible release; and wringing her dangled hands, she bowed herself over the sill, her mind circling downward like a plummet through a pit of misery, her body listening, as it were, to the pain of her breast crushed against the stone. "Ridiculous," she said to herself.

Meanwhile, she also had to think about her money. We can't talk about it, or I know she won't so I don't even try, but it's what goes unsaid between people that builds up like masonry. Tears brimmed up—there I go again, she said. To be continued. She talks about getting "my MFA," as if dropping by the school to pick up something she left there, maybe a coat.

Some situations brought out Eleanor's competence, and others touched the secret springs of her insecurity; her marriage did both. No one can explain exactly what happens within us when the doors behind which our childhood terrors lurk are flung open. She had no interest in men, particularly of the servile class. She was thirty-one years old, and had been married eight years. They had married quickly, for love. It was the moonlight that had weakened her, the moonlight and her own desire. His rosy tongue had vanquished her.

He and his sister, it was credibly believed, indulged in a little incest from time to time. His hatred of the vulgar and the mediocre found expression in sarcastic outbursts of superb lyricism, and he held the old masters in such veneration that it almost raised him to their level. Exalted but remote. Whenever he went out she was afraid that he would never come back; otherwise she was extraordinarily happy and hoped they would always be together. He was desperate to be a success—at anything, more or less. She had cried with rage, after he had left her, at—she hardly knew what: she tried to think it had been at his want of consideration.

After that she was rich and free. There was nothing to do but drink.

She walked on, pleased with the adventure, thinking that perhaps the only satisfactory way of life was to live for the minute.

I remarked in jest that he had surely found his man. (We had sex in the laundry room of his apartment building a few times.) I've never cultivated his society, and he apparently has never found mine indispensable to his happiness. Later she was unfaithful to him: openly; deliberately; defiantly.

If there was anything childish or demure about her as a bride, that soon vanished. "I had an awful love affair," she said, still weeping. She expected that I would disapprove. "Then I went home for the summer to Indiana." She looked at me blankly and then, little by little, almost imperceptibly, a smile, or the irrepressible prelude to a smile, slightly rearranged her features. Mentally, I rolled my eyes. I didn't love her, and she certainly didn't love me, but perhaps in a way we could have made a life together.

Alone unchanging are women's ambitions and men's desires.

৪০ 21 ୪

Something very strange is happening to me, every face I see seems to be smiling. You know what I mean when I say that. Desirelessness.

So one day my son was taking a nap and I was looking at the local free throwaway newspaper and I spotted a curious ad in the classifieds: a dominatrix with a transsexual assistant was offering $100 one-hour sessions.

"Do come in," she said, trying to sound gracious.

I make sure not to come out looking too damaged. It was like a victory.

The result is not the point; it is the effort to improve ourselves that is valuable.

Are you constantly conscious of the clock ticking?

How much time does love take? This is Freud's implicit question. It is some sort of defense against death.

Noon slumbers.

❧ 22 ☙

A high-class restaurant where everything is special. There, milling about, whirling around, flitting here and there, were the most beautiful women of Paris, the richest, the noblest, dazzling, stately, resplendent with diamonds, flowers in their hair, on their bosoms, on their heads, strewn over dresses or in garlands at their feet. People had to be looked at before being admitted, but everyone was always let in. The mostly faded wallpaper still showed a few traces of yellow. It was the first time I'd been to a place like that, such an expensive place, I mean, and I must admit a ravenous hunger possessed me all of a sudden, because although I'm as thin as a rake, put food in front of me and I'm liable to fall upon it like the Unrepentant Glutton of the Southern Cone, or the Emily Dickinson of Bulimia, especially if it's an assortment of cheeses to beggar belief and a variety of wines to set your head spinning. Champagne does wonders for boosting the morale, everyone knows that.

"But, what am I to do?" she said. Here we have, I believe, the only philosophical question of any merit whatsoever. Like all the women in the world, she wanted a real lover. Whereas what I want is someone to fuck. We all love to tell those we love that we love them, and to hear from them that we are loved—but as grownups we are not quite as sure we know what this means as we once were, when we were children and love was a simple thing. We sat for a moment in silence, and then the waiter delivered our meals.

"Listen, my dear," I said gently. "You mustn't be worried,

he will come back." Eleanor was silent for a moment. "To forgive, it is best to know as little as possible."

"Yes, I can imagine," she said dryly.

I was having a good time, I realized suddenly. "The ancients have a saying," I said. I wanted to seem like I was in the process of focusing in on something important. "What every man knows best about himself is how to masturbate. And I confess that I continue to masturbate with distressing regularity, despite the paltry satisfaction I derive. Essentially, we would like the world to repeat our fantasies, to give us a satisfaction we have already given ourselves. The whole point of marriage is repetition. It is only we humans who insist on entangling the spiritual with the physical, and although this insistence has unquestionably inspired prodigies of literature and music and art in general ever since we started to scratch away with those flints on the walls of our primeval caves, it has also played merry hell with our nervous systems. I disapprove of that, don't you? If you're going to do something, do it halfway."

Eleanor laughed. She stopped abruptly, like the player lifting the bow from the strings with a flourish. She gave a long, pleased-sounding *hmmm.* "I love this wallpaper." She is elegantly dressed, but still somehow tired by evening of the day's burdens.

Right now, finally, temporarily, again, we are everything to each other. All at once I felt naked, revealed, like someone just ripped a blanket off my sleeping body. Then something opened in me, briefly, frighteningly, as if a little window had been thrown open to a vast, far, dark, deserted plain. "My dear Eleanor, the riot is only in your own brain." Finally, much exasperated, I dropped the subject. "If you ever get married again, don't tell your husband *any*thing."

I don't know if you have ever dined with a vegetarian. She could sit so still, and feel the day slowly, richly changing to night. Ketchup on nearly everything. Neither of us is saying what the other wants to hear.

"Wouldn't you like to do something else?" she asks. She was one of those women who are not beautiful, but who are illumined when they smile or laugh, like a dark pool when the sun suddenly shines on it. "But I hate to leave." She is a mistress of misunderstanding. "I could use another drink," she says. "When I was twelve years old, my best friend's mother died of cancer."

It was a stormy night and the rain was blowing against the skylights and windows, giving the evening a rather eerie atmosphere.

ಬ 23 ಜ

I drank two bottles of Rioja last night while watching a 1962 videotape of Moira Orfei, queen of the Italian circus, dancing in sync with Mozart's "Là ci darem la mano." I've pulled a lot of stunts in my day, mostly of the sick sexual variety, but that summer I reached a new low. Now I am on the last half-emptied case and it is way past midnight. I flinched when I thought about it. Writing is a high calling exacting great labour and patience and a certain self-sacrifice from those who profess it.

This night was unique for a number of reasons. I sat still on the doorstep of abstraction. The dahlias were drooping with sleep. My father is there, moving softly in the dusky room. He arrived late, as usual. One of his eyes was larger than the other, giving his face a somewhat sarcastic expression. Understand that I use the word *father* in a loose sense. A father who is always leaving and never coming back.

Occultism is the metaphysic of dunces.

I have been brooding on the word *malignant*. Think of the most disgusting thing you can think of. That's corruption. From fifteen on one can begin to wonder about such a thing, along with eternity and clouds and beauty and faith. But how can we resist being suspicious of the language here? "Why am I reading this?" is a different question.

With history piling up so fast, almost every day is the anniversary of something awful.

These questions carry me over the border.

Should a homosexual be a good citizen? That's the thing I always want to know. If I had the luck, certain mornings, to give up my seat in the bus or subway to someone who obviously deserved it, to pick up some object an old lady had dropped and return it to her with a familiar smile, or merely to forfeit my taxi to someone in a greater hurry than I, it was a real red-letter day. "The hero is the people." The sooner the barbarians understand that the better. Jesus wept: and no wonder, by Christ.

No spirit exists.

I surprised myself with this realization and, disturbed, sat up in bed, switched the lamp on, and lit a cigarette.

I don't have time for philosophy. I could use a sister's counsel.

Summertime shudders quietly to its close. Four days pass, and not a sign of him. "I need some time alone," he whispered. This is not true. "If you get bored, take a few pills." Thanks for everything.

The solitude was very much my own, with a freshness to it like that of the first sweet air of the day, the air you breathe through a half-open window at dawn.

I want to hear your voice.

But nobody comes and I am left to my own resources.

❧ 24 ☙

Because Joe was a notoriously hard person to buy gifts for, I asked him what he wanted for Christmas.

Joe answered, "What do you mean? As compensation what for?" Joe demanded. Ignorant and lazy though he must have found us, he remained sweetness itself. "Come and sit here, dear," said Joe persuasively, patting the sofa at his side. He is the embodiment of resilience, joie de vivre, and possibility. "In a recent survey a group of old people were asked if they had any regrets about their lives, and the majority of them said they regretted that they had been so virtuous." Yes, he says, we are foolish, but we cannot be any other way so we may as well relax and live with it. The reasonable man, he insisted, achieves nothing. "You cannot train children to be good citizens of a state which you despise."

That, I think, is the right kind of attitude. As the nineteenth-century philosopher Friedrich Nietzsche would warn, "One should not try to surpass one's father in diligence; that makes one sick."

He was soon writing Eleanor again. For too many years he had closed his eyes to Eleanor's activities, but now he would make it his business to take more than a casual interest. "I do hope you're having a wonderful time, darling," he wrote.

A letter from Eleanor followed. She felt that Joe was surely being destroyed. "Come to Spain with me, end of September," said Eleanor brisk and practical. "You know, Joe," she said,

"I don't mind what you do, if you love me *really*. Women are not like men." There is, I believe, something just the tiniest bit smug in that statement. "What about this father of yours?"

The next day the bitch came. Her gaiety had returned. She behaved flawlessly. "Hello, sweetheart. You see I did as you asked me to," she said. "As you know, I do my best to please you." I doubted that. "All my life I've done everything to excess:" that was her motto, and her method. Certainly there was arrogance in this attitude. Maybe a chemical imbalance is the root to her bitchiness. For Eleanor, the racket and disorder, the weariness of constant travel, were bad enough, but the meals were the worst trial of all.

Presently the lad stood in front of her, wildly excited. She said a few words to him in Yiddish.

That is when he leans forward and kisses her. He was still a little spellbound by gaudiness. She is absurdly young, hardly twenty years older than he is, and seems all the time to be getting younger, or at least not older, so that he has the worrying sensation of steadily catching up on her. A dim antagonism gathered force within him and darkened his mind as a cloud against her disloyalty: and when it passed cloudlike leaving his mind serene and dutiful towards her again he was made aware dimly and without regret of a first noiseless sundering of their lives.

Her eyes, however, saw nothing; they had suddenly been suffused with tears.

But Joe said it didn't matter and made her sit down by the fire. He has a distressing habit of saying quietly to those with whom he is familiar the most shocking things about himself and others, and, moreover, of selecting the most shocking times for saying them, not because they are shocking merely, but because they are true.

"I need a drink," he said. The more clearly he saw, the more cunning he grew.

"Yes," she sighed, subsiding. "So there'll be two drunks instead of one." Strange words to be speaking over breakfast, over coffee and toast.

"Look here," he said. "A person's a person, no matter how small." So adult did he look in the depth of his meditation that she could not resist smiling. Then, on a sudden but apparently pressing impulse, he stretched out supine on the carpet. The ways of women will never cease to perplex him. This was a case of metaphysics, at least as difficult for Joe to deal with, as for me. "I just can't take it no more," he said. "She thinks I'm going to stay on here forever just being a boy." We have heard this kind of talk before.

Later Joe was to ascribe his acquiescence to his desire to please, to be accepted and loved, but it was due also to his being what was then called a "sissy." He was one of those sensitive beings who blush guiltily when someone else makes a blunder. He's a funny kid. Normality is a precarious condition. But many things that are disposed of in the minds of grownups are not yet settled in the minds of the young. Inadequate as he felt himself to be in the practical skills of life, he knew the advantage he had when it came to literature and learning. His waking hours were spent in a prison of rituals and superstitions, his "mania," as he called it.

Time would take care of the situation. But few people will love him, I think, in spite of his graces and his genius and whosoever exchanges kindnesses with him is likely to get the worst of the bargain. "Oh, I know that," he said softly, in a tone of intimate contempt. Joe shuffled down the carpeted stairs still in his pajamas. "Let me deceive myself." Going upstairs, the sole of one of his slippers monotonously slapped the bare boards. "Dad understands that."

"Why should I?" she replied, and blew her nose. "That's just what I don't want, Joe." This rings absolutely true, proving that sloth often alters truth more than mere mendacity.

Even as they spoke the sun was beginning to disappear behind a cloud. Her influence over him was gone. He was destined to learn his own wisdom apart from others or to learn the wisdom of others himself wandering among the snares of the world. Eleanor did not dispute this. "He was born an old man, that's how it started." How can they know each other so little, after all this time? She builds an imaginative life that will shut out the real, and she has done this since childhood.

Eleanor's view prevailed. It was life but was it fair?

Silence.

Now that's what I call a breakfast.

ༀ 25 ༚

"Well, this would interest you. There is a woman in China, twenty-nine years old, whose right foot is on her left leg."

David closed his eyes and pictured it. "Life has been difficult for her," he said. "Sounds dreadful." He was smoking a pipe, and his feet, in silk socks and red leather slippers, were resting on a footstool. He was freshly shaved and this gave his face a thin, pure beauty. And it begins to look very old-fashioned. Style is an extraordinary thing. I turned on the radio as I cooked. Nothing and everything happening at once. "Chopin, eh?" It was Stravinsky. Despite everything that has happened, and everything I desired to happen that never did, I can still soothe myself with this kind of music. Messages from an unvisited island. And then there's the food. To cook is not just to prepare food for someone or for yourself; it is to express your sincerity.

How much my life has changed, and yet how unchanged it has remained at bottom! Every moment it seems to me that I am running away from myself.

At this moment David appeared as if by magic. "Darling, is there any Perrier in the fridge?" he said, removing a pill from his little box. To this crucial question I answer with a resounding yes. "Oh God," he said, "I'm late again." Every time he raised his eyes and saw the beauty of the country in the failing light he wanted to do something he had never done before, shout or scream or hit his wife with his fists or something equally unexpected and terrifying.

He is ill-mannered, self-preoccupied, austere—the modern psychologists would probably diagnose him as introverted, narcissistic and manic depressive. Seen from a more sympathetic angle, the picture is quite different. He tops, for one thing, and sometimes when he gets frisky he gets rough.

I consider my thoughts, my frail fucked-up memory. It is made of details. Just a few years ago I learned from my mother that my father always suspected, with reason, that I was another man's offspring. And that's what all this is a little bit about. That's just the way: a person does a low-down thing, and then he don't want to take no consequences of it. How was it that I did not know? You're always hearing about these kinds of kinks in royal families. Such are the phantoms we create out of each other.

There are moments when we find it astonishing, this life.

In the real world things were going along about as well as could be expected, that is, not quite satisfactorily. I remember that the days and nights passed like bars of white and black, opening and shutting. But, in all, so vibrant.

To be is a verb.

David, at the kitchen door, caught his breath chokingly. "Do you want to hear something funny? I came here to quit drinking," he said, and tears began to run down his cheeks. *Funny* is almost certainly not the right word. David was one of those men of intense feeling who thrust their sufferings deep down and hide them from those who are dear to them, so that when grief overflows, as his did now, they have reached the limit of endurance. "Is it naïve of me in my antiquated way to think that people should do what they say they're going to do?" He kissed my neck, and sniffed my hair. "I cannot tell to what level I may sink."

Indeed, I thought to myself, *the spirit can't go wrong if there's no spirit to begin with.*

He began to giggle through his tears. But in a special way. "I was once a man," he said, "but now I'm not." This had never happened before. Is he just spouting 12-step truisms he's picked up God knows where? "I was not joking, my dear; so tell me why you did not come last night." David was radically incapable of ill-humour for more than a few seconds at a time, and grinned in a less awful manner.

"David, you are being contrary and disingenuous, and just a little hostile, and I'm really not sure why."

"I'm beginning to hate myself."

Is that not the ambition of most young gentlemen?

David smiles, shyly showing me a photo of a very handsome tough guy who so personifies David's type. How well I'm getting to know these characters! David had been a "model" himself.

"Fertilize your inner life," I said.

"Shall we speak in everyday language? Who wrote

this dialogue?"

Dinner was not a success. Far from it. To put it in two words: disaster struck. He suffered tortures of humiliation and self-consciousness. From there on it got worse. I left him sitting there wishing he was dead. The end of everything was at hand; it seemed to him he could stretch out his arm and touch the goal. Something must be wrong with us.

He selected a pair of blue pajamas and put them on with care, smoothing the wide collar and sticking a dainty blue silk handkerchief in the little patch pocket over his left breast. "I know how much you idolize the rich."

And so the lovely music glided to its glowing close.

I will not serve that in which I no longer believe whether it call itself my home, my fatherland or my church: and I will try to express myself in some mode of life or art as freely as I can and as wholly as I can, using for my defence the only arms I allow myself to use, silence, exile and cunning.

But the Milky Way, it seemed to me, was still the same tattered streamer of star-dust as of yore. That is the truly devastating message of this book. That is how the past exists, phantasmagoric weskits, stray words, random things recorded. It is too late to be yourself. Writing is no longer possible.

Too late.

Of all the vices there are, there is one we cannot permit

ourselves, and that is patience.

The light that reveals us to ourselves is always inconvenient.

No man knows what dangers he should avoid from one hour to another.

❧ 26 ☙

All my life I have been what is traditionally regarded as an amusing person, and this capacity to be amusing was often the label I displayed to the world or the flag I sailed under. It called for strength, courage, and physical élan, all things that I lacked. The psychologists know all about this. But I'm very peaceful, momentarily, this evening. I don't want fanfare.

One thing is undeniable. Given how our mouths tend to fill up with other people's speech, the struggle not to become a mere ventriloquist's dummy is not only a concern for mediocre writers.

A friend of mine, an English teacher at a local university, says he feels an obligation to point out to his students that the cigars in the canister on the mantelpiece in an Edith Wharton story are phallic symbols. The fairies broke into animated discussion.

Life mirrors art.

This tickles Joe to pieces. "He must have been pontificating like crazy."

What other point of view could there be? Life in New York was pleasant in those days. "And I want to live a quiet life there," I said, the blunt tone of my own voice ringing in my ears. My conscience pricked me. I wanted to write enormous naturalistic novels with unhappy endings, full of detailed descriptions and arresting similes, and also full of purple passages in which words were used partly for the sake of their sound. And I can never really forget that voluptuousness and volition share the same etymological origin.

❧ 27 ☙

I must have slept for a long time. David was sitting up, and he immediately fixed his eyes on me. Had they remained still for any length of time his eyes would have been kind; as it was he looked kind of anxious. As he had nothing to do, his idleness intensified his melancholy.

"I suffer every night," I said, "from amorous dreams which wear me out." It takes ages.

To which David: "Is that why you are so kind to me?" I think that follows, Socrates. He is tortured by future anguish.

My real type, these days, is a blue-collar closet queen— they're the best.

Meaning is never monogamous. But in the realm of sex, more than in any other area of human life, shame rules. It hurts.

I don't know how much more pathetic I can become.

David sighs. "Turn over here and let me look at you," he ordered softly. He puts on a queer smile. "Maybe you're ready to ease up on the Demerol." He lay on a cot next to the open window, and he was naked except for a pink brassiere and a pair of yellow panties. He's a man who won't stop talking.

"Go to hell," I said. This is the punishment, I thought, now you have your reckoning.

To me the most astonishing phenomenon is not the power-man's desire to dominate but the human craving to believe— if not in Man—in a man. We never release ourselves from him, his voice, his sense—from one moment to the next—of living a life bruised, embittered, ironic, superior, passive, aggressive, punitive, erotic, whimpering.

At any rate, it was definitely thumbs down. I had to get out of there and have sex as quickly as possible.

ཚ 28 ༒

The cocks are getting ready to say good morning to the sun. It is like the beginning of a beautiful day. Christmas was approaching.

Joe slept on our living-room couch. He hears nothing of what you shout and overhears everything you whisper. This was a habit that exasperated his mother; he knew it and she knew he knew it. Like many people who are thought antisocial, he was not aloof because he was indifferent or antipathetic, but because he was so profoundly affected by others that he could not easily locate the boundaries between their expectations and his own.

"You don't know him," David exclaimed. He had his grand manner on. "I wish we could sometimes hear some positive praise of our little boy." This, he insisted, would be solace. "Poor boy! he's got to live," David asserted with the humility of an employer who feels that he himself is to blame. "You won't believe what he's got me doing."

At the risk of unwarranted ghoulishness, I cannot suppress a final irony. David drank slowly but steadily whenever possible. He was a man doomed to suffer. It had brought out the worst in him, and no one saw this more clearly than Eleanor. The Romantic is nearly always a rebel. Etc., etc., etc. I suppose it is easy to understand how this topic can become such a volatile one. The sex with him was pure sorcery as always, but there was a new element in it of savagery and despair, and more than once I got a sharp disturbing whiff of awful finality in his actions. Desire was his crime, he saw.

Seeing Dick Cheney looming up on the television screen with that weird lust in his eyes and bits of brain matter in the cracks of his teeth might accidentally be diagnosed as dementia. Joe and I gasped, and looked at one another. Television is a mystery. The vivid rhetoric of terror was a first step in the slow process toward American Democracy. "Don't lose your temper," said Joe. "He should have come out of the closet years ago like everybody else, and then he wouldn't have to do all that compensating." You took the words out of my mouth. I'm getting so I can't bear the sight of newspapers. Joyce is right about history being a nightmare—but it may be the nightmare from which no one *can* awaken. History makes me numb.

I thought: "My son will be hurt." I am all emptiness and futility. There is no such thing as inner peace.

Must be the war news.

It's right before Christmas, and I'm feeling very anxious.

"Dad," he says. "Don't worry."

"O.K., O.K." I do not see you as you really are, Joseph; I see you through my affection for you.

My dear child, your father will need you.

෨ 29 ෫

David introduced me to a man named Roy Hardeman. He was not good-looking, but his policeman's uniform, and the idea that he was a policeman, excited me. It was a new, glamorous world. In all things, it is the beginnings and ends that are interesting. Or was I wrong about that?

I stared at him, holding my breath. He was tall and strongly built, his face rather pale. He had a huge hairless head. In his left ear he wore a gold earring: a snake swallowing its tail. He's a former pro boxer, and once had a fight in Mississippi where he kicked his opponent in the scrotum when he couldn't conquer him with his fists, then wept tears of frustration.

For all I know he may be a prince in disguise; he rather looks like one, by the way—like a prince who has abdicated in a fit of fastidiousness and has been in a state of disgust ever since. Perhaps the man was the less handsome for the deep lines in his face, the irritable tension of his brow, which gave him the look of a man who fights with life. He also struck me as a rather cruel man, although it would have been difficult for me to say why. The handshake of some people makes you think of accident and sudden death. There are some people who invariably make a favorable first impression.

A single insight at the start is worth more than ever so many somewhere in the middle.

As a child, he had been raised by his grandparents, and been allowed to run wild. And so on. He was one of those young men whose age is difficult to determine. His bald head sits solemnly on the brown plinth of his neck. He stared at me with such interest that I could only feel flattered.

The signs of some incurable gastric disorder were written all over his sour face. There was a very definite smell of fish and chips.

"I suppose I'm a little disturbed. I was just brushing my teeth and about to go to bed," I explained, nervously. A bitch, of course....

David said he was sorry. Dandruff dusted the lapels of his Jacket.

"David, what is Tofrinal, that I see it in the medicine chest, a big bottle full?"

The young man said something wonderful in response. "David told me how hard you work in the garden you made, and the way you love all the flowers." His voice was like his look: dull and proud. He uses a language, has a way of speaking, that instantly made me think: inimical to civilization.

"Ah, they're part of the comedy." Sometimes not so comic. "It's regrettable, but that's the way it is. Oh, honey, don't let me *commence.*" So alone, in this galaxy of fairies.

"We met on a plane," David said.

Ridiculous. He went from going to bed with handsome people to going to bed with ordinary people, and finally ugly men; with Jews, Italians, Slavs and Brazilians, Dutchmen, Germans, Greeks and Arabs. Our flesh shrinks from what it dreads and responds to the stimulus of what it desires by a purely reflex action of the nervous system. But the fear of going too far, and that of not going far enough, robbed him of all power of judgment. Being full of lust and hatred, envy and deceit, his desires are insatiable. I don't pretend to be a judge of these things, but I thought the effect exaggerated and not in the best of taste. There is no bad taste—only taste and no taste. He has become a wolf. Drinking, unfortunately, can make the symptoms worse. It is a horrible thing to feel that all that we possess is draining away.

Oh, dear, I am so tired of feeling spiteful, but how else is one to feel? The measure of your loyalty is the reluctance you feel to give up an attachment for an attraction. But, dear David, enough of this is enough. "You wicked boy!" I said.

Some time was spent looking for a subject of conversation. "His wife is in France." My eyes fill with tears as I think of her. While his soul had passed from ecstasy to languor where had she been? Even now, after years of marriage, they foundered on the same gloomy psychological shoals every time they made love. "He's living with a young Japanese girl." So I think he must have felt quite an acute sense of discomfort in France. Perhaps.

And homesick is where, when you go home, they make you sick.

It was interesting to see the concentration in David's face. What was his purpose in doing this? He seemed to be considering having a heart attack. I remember everything right down to the last detail. I found his drunkenness scary and appealing since he wasn't quite himself.

"What do I have to do to make you want to live with me again?" I asked. There should have been background music. "I'm not recommending it, I'm just asking."

"I couldn't do that, I just couldn't," he said with a feckless sigh.

"You are sleeping with me to-night, you know, David," I said. "I love you." When God hands you a gift, he also hands you a whip; and the whip is intended solely for self-flagellation. But not David's. "Well, I mean, it's Christmas..." I segue into the vanity of human attachment. Inconstancy, boredom, anxiety. This estrangement is a recent phenomena [sic]. "I'll give you just ten seconds to wipe that stupid grin off of your face."

"Now, just wait a second, sonny," he said. David beams, showing me a photo of a hillbilly trucker with a giant dick. "I'm sure you can find plenty of other people to talk to." But there he was probably wrong. What better way of assuring oneself, on the point on which one is mistaken, than to persuade the other of the truth of what one says! "I wish you'd learn to leave the goddam party when it's over," he said. He was happiest and most truly himself when he was alone in the quiet countryside.

I watched them for as long as I could, until they disappeared, two shrinking forms, around a corner. Like lightning they were gone. But what do they have in common?

"Every son loves his father," I said, getting into bed. One is inclined to say so. "Joe needs you to look after him." He could not be entirely alone.

I thought of my garden. We used to have picnics. To the east there was a belt of trees, warped and stunted by the wind from the sea.

But soon I fell smack into sleep and did not dream any more. Why not?

ಬಿ 30 ಲ

I have returned to reality! It's expensive, but it's wonderful therapy. It has a certain reckless glory, such as the Greeks loved.

The awareness that you are here, right now, is the ultimate fact.

But nothing is ever quite the same the second time around. Everywhere I turned, a cruel and lurid world surged around me. Twenty-first century America is in a state of decline.

I refuse to be entirely absent. There, I always thought, is a major hole in my character.

This clearer view of things lent a gelatinous cast to my morning questions about an "inner life" that I might comfortably do without.

"It's all very fine talking," muttered Joe, who had been fidgeting in his chair with divers uneasy gestures. "Aren't you bored?" He is rarely petulant or fretful, even with his boredom. The older I grow, and the better I get to know him, the more I love him.

Love for a woman or girl is not to be compared to a man's love for an adolescent boy.

A curious sea side feeling in the air today. An atmosphere of unusual relaxation had spread over the house. If I had books here I'd read. A "feel bad" book always makes me feel good.

Reading is like entering a hall of mirrors.

It was the severe presence of the sea which made the rather ugly house romantic. Climatically speaking, we have every reason to expect the worst.

Years ago I asked the critic Elizabeth Hardwick if her divorce from poet Robert Lowell had been in any way difficult. You must admit, I said to her, that it would be hard to concoct a more instructive tale: two bewildered profligates condemned to nauseating one another. "Ha ha ha," she said. She drained her vodka. "I liked him," she said. "People can say what they like but breeding will tell. Adversity has its advantages." The notion of happiness no longer seems to be in fashion.

I am not wandering at random, I have a goal, but I pass it by, often and on purpose. In other words, it's all a question of technique. Mental confusion is not always chaos.

Human communication, it sometimes seems to me, involves an exaggerated amount of time. It's always late.

"Want to guess what I heard about Roy?"

"What?" Joe said, looking over at me. He lay back relaxed in his favorite chair. What does it look like, he wonders, when you kiss someone, as the other's face comes towards your own, until it dissolves into an unfocused blur, and your experience of it necessarily shifts, becomes one of touch and taste rather than of sight?

"Her father," I said, "is a Polish Jew." We only laugh at those with whom we feel we have an affinity that we must repudiate, that we feel threatened by.

The youth became serious; his triangular face assumed an unexpectedly manly look. "I met him for the first time yesterday. Unbearable. He kept asking me if I wanted a ride on his motorcycle. He says a boy ought to know how to do things like that. I acted bored so as not to show how excited I was. To face up to death is to see your life as a finite project, something that can and will be finished. Funny, I'm not particularly happy about it. What I need is criticism—savage criticism." It is a fundamentally insane notion, he continues, that one is able to influence the course of events by a turn of the helm, by will-power alone, whereas in fact all is determined by the most complex interdependencies. And yet here he was, his father's son in the only way that really mattered.

We are drinking iced mint tea slightly flavored with absinthe. Intellectually we were unprepared—and I was perhaps less prepared than anyone—to come to grips with the tasks that confronted us. The tasks would be too complex.

How to avoid suicide? Opting out of the system may have been one solution, like a brilliant friend of mine who'd suddenly decided, after a motorbike accident, to give up his social life, as though his head had cleared during his convalescence and he'd suddenly, joyfully, been set free, veering away from people forever, just as he'd skidded euphorically off the road, and he never looked back. Desire is the enemy of the ego, not its expression. It is a characteristic of our species, in evolutionary terms, that we are a species in despair, for a number of reasons. "Forget it, Joe. Let's discuss *you*." But that didn't happen.

"Efen if zey offered me millions, I voult not say von vort! Adultery's more fun," he said with attempted lightness. "So David tells me. May we now be permitted to enter slightly into this difficult and dark region?" Joe was not given to subtle maneuvering such as this, but who knows? This the way to the museyroom. It was already midnight. Full moon sends rapid clouds dashing past a cold sky. I wanted to go to sleep for ever. I groaned and closed my eyes to try to shut out my tormentor, but Joe was never one to give up easily. "I've got something to tell you, Dad. Love amazes, but it does not surprise. The most precious thing in life is its uncertainty."

"Not for long," I said.

Joe listed one reason. A dissatisfied mind, whatever else it may miss, is rarely in want of reasons; they bloom as thick as buttercups in June. He wished he had never learned who his father was. "So is this really Christmas?" he thought.

"I've had my share of uncertainty and you cannot blame me if I do not want to see the worst side of it reproduced in you." I don't know whether I succeed in expressing myself, but I know that nothing else expresses me. "No, freedom is better! I think all theories are suspect, that the finest principles may have to be modified, or may even be pulverized by the demands of life, and that one must find, therefore, one's own moral center and move through the world hoping that this center will guide one aright. I took my last ride on a motorcycle, believe me. Finally, in all your preparations, *begin as you mean to go on."*

"Oui, oui, c'est ça, c'est magnifique!" He chewed, and said: "I can't remember what I wanted to say, but I know it was something malicious."

Nothing is easy until you do it every day.

"Quietly, my son," I whisper.

At eighteen minutes to four we heard the rustle of David's wings. "I am leaving you," he said. "You must find someone else."

Nonsense. Non c'è peggior sordo di chi non vuol sentire. No one is so deaf as he who will not hear.

I laughed in a certain way, because I could not speak. He was gone. There remains only the one consolation that nobody knows where he is.

Will our shame never end?

It was all offensive, but I found myself the most offensive of all.

ಬ 31 ಆ

But after all, the winter did end. The city and its parks became leafy, billowing green even while morning frost clung to the windows. On one of the handful of nights I've ventured out and away from the typewriter in the weeks of writing this book, I strolled through my favorite haunts in Central Park and met up with a fine, sensitive man who was into talking, as I was. The mating of minds is, surely, quite as fascinating a relationship as the mating of the sexes, yet how little attention novelists have paid to it. With fallen branches, as dry and brittle as chalk, and some dead leaves gathered from the crevices, I made us a bedding, where we half reclined and talked. The chords geese behind us honked tingled like seltzer. Of all the heavenly bodies only the moon, hanging almost full above the Hilton Hotel, was visible.

"I believe Tarkovsky expressed his intent very well on the screen," I said. He looked at me, perplexed. I felt for the first time I was speaking for myself. "My mother was a Freudian. It was cooler than anything else. I was never raped— except nearly—once. Some three years ago," I recounted, "I happened to be bathing beside a young man, blessed at the time with an astounding beauty. Since then I've had a terrible fondness for asses. It was a strange coincidence," I said. Encountering a stranger brings one into contact with the unconscious. "Which reminds me of a story from those years that may be worth telling. Any congruence with reality is delightful. On the high school track team, I often stopped to walk. Competition is a sublimation of warfare." This was disingenuous. "And I'm speaking of a twelve-year-old boy, not some grownup who has had the time to ripen a naturally evil disposition. Nevertheless, not everyone was amused. Though I would not wish to return to that lost innocence if I could—to live impaled, who needs it? To this day I cannot understand myself, and it has all floated by like a dream—even my passion—it was violent and sincere, but . . . what has become of it now? In all my childhood only one perception ever seemed to me now, in hindsight, as having been, to use that beautiful word, lucid: the sense that struck me once at day camp, that the people and places all around me, everything in short, was just an elaborate hoax, made up of actors and sets—I didn't know whether to be more surprised by the scope of the thing (no doubt serving some secret purpose that was, unfortunately, beyond me) or by its low budget (which would explain the bad architecture and the extras' general lack of talent), and even if I understood this wasn't literally true, still it was a striking and conclusive glimpse of the fraudulence that surrounded me. And is the truth less meaningless than lies? Human sensitivity to little things and insensitivity to the greatest things: sign of a strange disorder."

"Would you please please please please please please please stop talking?" Nothing but disdain. The man with the cruel look in his eyes who is interrogating me suddenly starts coughing. As a boy he was abandoned by his mother and raised by peasants in an impoverished part of France. Clearly the story meant much to him. He had a beautiful voice with a Bronx accent. He has enormous pectoral breasts, which must further endear him to the gay community. But he never got to fuck anybody. He squeezes me tight for a few endless seconds. The slow pressing of flesh against flesh was more intimate to me than a passionate kiss would have been. You can feel him saying, My god, how lucky I am, and alas, how old I am. It occurred to me that I might be making a mistake. What is going to happen? We're deep into the night. "No," he said, "I don't want to see your son. I am, as you may observe, no longer young, and what I haven't seen of life isn't worth seeing. You should have become either a tough villain or a tough angel, one or the other." God approved his every thought. "Yes, I know you don't like me, but I'll go with you all the same." No matter how fantastic or excited his speech, he never changed his expression.

The man had no idea of what he wanted, and I made him aware of this in the most forceful way; I said that what he was doing was morbid, that his whole life was a morbid life, his existence a morbid existence, and consequently everything he was doing was irrational, if not utterly senseless. "No. Your Highness, I find to my amazement that this highly informative discussion has exceeded the time we had allowed for it." The white American regards his darker brother through the distorting screen created by a lifetime of conditioning. "You have beautiful hair," I said.

"Wait a second," the man says. A breeze was slightly disturbing his hair. "You're not an Italian, are you?"

That isn't funny, it's just vulgar. It was high time to go. "Time to fuck off." Filth: it is inseparable from sex, from its essence. Just how he could manage to face his wife and two children twenty minutes after was not my problem, of course.

Then for a time I stumbled about in a cold darkness. My

belly is warm and happy, though full of wind. To live beyond forty is indecent, banal, immoral!

But as I walked down the steps I saw that the evening was not quite over. Eleanor, and only Eleanor, stood there. She was like a statue that embodied universal carnage and, at the same time, was unconcerned with the effects of that carnage; she came to represent heedlessness itself—in her, heedlessness had reached its heights of perfect oblivion. It was very strange. She looks as uncanny as ever, and more severe as she gets older. She was sort of gorgeous. "I don't know, dear," she said, "but I think the scenery's so perfectly French." Not true. She was cold, and tired, and ageing, and disgraced. Six years of virtue and security had almost tamed her.

"What are you doing?" I asked. "My life lately is full of coincidences."

She put both hands on my shoulders, and looked at me intently; she seemed trying to read something in my face. "You like being mysterious, don't you?" She is so practiced in her self-deceptions that she can make convincing arguments on their behalf. "You get along very well without me."

"Oh yes," I said. Quite so. Cowed by my tone, she backed away a few steps. Her mouth was slightly open—she could feel that—and waves of horripilation fled across her skin. She was a little vulgar; some times she said "I seen" and "If I had've known." I wanted to kiss her. I was elated; and I walked in front feeling very gay.

She wasn't sure yet, but she certainly thought her life needed a lift. But we were sure it was not a thing we wanted to think about. "You don't want me here, do you?" she said. She felt a surprising pleasure. With an impulse that borders on the religious, she's searching for truth. She wants to be loved, she wants to be admired, she wants to be a success, she wants to give others pleasure, she wants to stay young. She had a hard, bright devil inside her, that she seemed to be able to let loose at will.

"Actually your father did once mention a strain of insanity in his family."

In the darkness beyond she heard a rustle and the sound of something breathing, the noise of some startled animal making off.

All is mystery except our pain.

We lust for apocalypse.

ॐ 32 ∞

Surprisingly, Eleanor journeyed to England in the autumn. And throughout the journey she practiced herself in the mood she must take and keep: a mood cool, artful, and determined. From early morning till about three o'clock in the afternoon she would seldom speak—it taking that time to thaw her, by all accounts, into but talking terms with humanity. Those who thought they best knew her, often wondered what happiness such a being could take in life, not considering the happiness which is said to be had by some natures in the very easy way of simply causing pain to those around them. In short she was fast becoming more uninhibitedly herself than ever.

༄ 33 ༀ

The forsythia is spent now, but there are lilacs, azaleas, geraniums, Japanese wisteria.

And you as you always were.

Do you remember?

I read again these notebooks. To this end I am at present staying for a few days at a hotel. The pleasures of obsession. In the vicinity of the hotel the lights of luxury apartments loomed insolently.

The very writing of my book of memoirs had brought home to me that memory is a darkroom for the development of fictions.

"Language," says Wittgenstein, "sets everyone the same traps; it is an immense network of easily accessible wrong turnings...." (Uttering a word is like striking a note on the keyboard of the imagination.) There is no one reason why people talk. In short, all my reading was coming in handy.

For no reason at all I looked at myself in the mirror for a long time; I was horribly unkempt, almost coarse, with swollen features that were not even ugly, and the rank look of a man just out of bed. A writer without his own tone is no writer at all. It's scarcely possible for the artist to write a word (or render an image or make a gesture) that doesn't remind him of something already achieved.

We are in fact made of the same material as Isabel Archer, as Dorothea Brooke.

A novel must be new and not new.

"Once you pick up a Compton-Burnett," Ivy commented about her own books, "it's hard *not* to put them down again."

ರಿ 34 ଔ

Roy gets up off his knees when he sees me. "Be sober," he admonished himself. This succeeded, to his own astonishment. When he got to his feet finally, shaking his head and staggering a little, all he could say was, "My God! That it should come to this! "

He sat down on a bench, unceremoniously, doggedly, like a man in trouble; leaning his elbows on his knees and staring at the floor. A bold, blunt-tipped nose, positive chin, a very large mouth,--the lips thick and succulent but never loose, never relaxed, always stiffened by effort or working with excitement. Never as a young man had he imagined himself at thirty-four. He'd grown up in the Pentecostal faith and had been frightened by the old people speaking in tongues every Sunday. He gets up, dresses, says his prayers, and sits down to his breakfast: he drinks three glasses of tea and eats two large doughnuts, and half a buttered French roll. So far so good. "Every thing must have a beginning . . . and that beginning must be linked to something that went before."

Don't be too hard on him, he was studying to be a professor. And he retained a Brooklyn pronunciation: his 'the' tended to be 'duh,' 'with' to be 'wit,' 'working' to be 'woiking.' We came to like him, to trust him, almost to admire him. He wrote a novel. But is a man capable of self-understanding? We take almost all the decisive steps in our lives as a result of slight inner adjustments of which we are barely conscious. He said one of the ways to compose is to go over what you're doing and see if it still works as you add something else to it. "You should write as a writer would, polish it up, embellish, add some style to it, that's your job, as far as I know." The most important key in the world is passed on from one sleepwalker to another.

When I squint I can see that the small bookshelf propped on the desk holds volumes by Freud, Winnicott, Lacan. The room was a maze of little objects and curiosities, arranged somewhat in the manner of a Woolworth's bargain window.

Tell me, what became of you?

The policeman replies, "I don't know. I've only one ambition—to be free to follow out a good feeling. Fashion is very important to me. For this alone I consider myself a very lucky man. I learned that just beneath the surface there's another world, and still different worlds as you dig deeper. We must learn to what extent our thoughts are consistent with our lives, and to what extent compensatory; to what extent ideals are a guide to behaviour, and to what extent they are behaviour itself."

The young man was certainly a windbag, and might be a rival. Not bad, but—how can I put it?—a little odd. He would describe for you the empire waist and puff-capped sleeves, and with his forefinger he might languidly draw a semicircle just below his collarbone to show you what he meant by a scooped neck. His words sounded low, in a sad murmur as of running water; at times they rang loud like the clash of a war-gong—or trailed slowly like weary travelers—or rushed forward with the speed of fear. The style, as always, tells the deep story. The names of articles of dress worn by women or of certain soft and delicate stuffs used in their making brought always to his mind a delicate and sinful perfume. We stand at opposite ends of the kitchen, two naked men, first not looking at each other, then looking.

"Well, my very earliest childhood memory was on the scary side. I wasn't in a mood for people in those days. Must I remember? I ended by finding sacred the disorder of my intelligence. . . . Nothing contagious," I assured him. Fictions constructed out of quotations--. "What is that you are eating?" I shout. There was salami, sliced hard-boiled eggs, lambs' tongues, cold ham and roast beef, potato salad, cheese and fresh figs.

"You said so many things, and I've forgotten all of them. What foolishness!" His lips were strong and yet gentle as he spoke.

Enough, unhappy one, I said, be still.

❧ 35 ☙

It was a sunny day. Wild spring. A pack of teenagers kept up an ecstatic dance of their own. There was great variety in their faces, but in nearly all something supercilious and sardonic. I hate them. Yet they looked not so much sinister as desperately sad. It feels like a massive gang rape is about to take place and we're all the rapists and the victims at the same time. It goes on forever. All night their voices rose and fell, sharpening into quarrels like the voices of men.

Let them howl. It is an event of great power and beauty in its ferocity. Perhaps it is the spirits who write my stories.

The telephone rings.

"Well, thank you for calling, David. I'm tired of hearing myself talk."

"It is essential to be occupied. It is a great art and I have mastered it. From tomorrow onwards," said David, "I shall only be able to go out at night." It seems to him that people are stopping in the street, following him with their eyes, as if to say: there he is at last. "Who is there to fuck around here? The police officer?"

Again I had to confess my ignorance. "I'll be right over," I said. "But you're not in New York, are you?" O Mary, go and call the cattle home / For I'm sick in my heart and fain would lie down.

"The arrangement," David notes laconically, "sounded very promising, so we decided to go. There was a man there called a *folk*-singer," says David with venom, "and, naturally, everybody had to hear some *folk* songs." At dinner he didn't realize the girls sitting at the next table were boys. "And this guy says, 'I don't care if it's the fucking queen of England!'"

"A poet, I dare say." It is two o'clock in the morning. I have nothing to say.

What if you had got a son, and the copy showed the same flaws as the original? I suffered from wrestling with the trap that I had thoughtlessly led myself into.

He tells of a kind of love affair. "I did not know we had friends in common," he said.

Now at this most inappropriate of times my sex begins to reassert itself. That was the root of the trouble! So I drank and smoked, drank and smoked. The secret duel had now begun.

Oh, how undignified this was!

"I have been trying to remember you as you were before all this happened," I say. The deepest history is the history of subjectivity. The past is consumed in the present and the present is living only because it brings forth the future.

For an evening or two I experience a quiet, fickle sadness, before I begin to forget.

ೞ 36 ೪

"It's because"—Joe caught his breath—"like the book puts it: 'Whosoever shall say unto this mountain be thou removed into the sea an'—uh-uh, yeah—'an' shall not doubt that those things which he hath sayeth shall come to pass, why, man, that guy is gonna have just exactly what he sayeth!'" He was leaning over the table, his hands clenching it, and trembling. As it happened, Joe had a truly sardonic sense of the absurd, and he was—as I would later learn—a deeply humane person. "God seeks people, good people, of course, he doesn't need the wicked and capricious—especially the capricious, who decide one thing today and say something else tomorrow." Perhaps this willingness to question certainties and prejudices just ran in the family. "I notice that scholars always manage to dig out something belittling," he complained. It felt like an episode in a dream, arbitrary and drenched with emotion.

Youth is a dreadful condition, I thought. He has a way of making everything I do seem unimportant. I turned away and straightened the unmade bed. I wobble a bit when I stand. He was right. It is not true that there is dignity in all work. Everyday life, with its duties and routines, was something I endured, not a thing I enjoyed, nor something that was meaningful or that made me happy.

"To the Renaissance!" he kept shouting.

That sort of thing is all right up to a certain age, no doubt, but if something isn't done to divert him, there is a good danger of his developing into a long-haired and anaemic ascetic.

"Just because it's Italian doesn't automatically mean it's valuable."

How many people have had so understanding a father?

"Pah!" cried Joe, in deep disgust. There are perhaps no days of our childhood we lived so fully as those we believe we left without having them, those we spent with a favorite book. "And she ain't over partial to having scholars on the premises," Joe continued, "and in partickler would not be over partial to my being a scholar, for fear as I might rise."

Quoting gets on my nerves.

Childhood seldom interests me at all. Had he been suppressing it? He began to wake in the night; the worried thoughts which came disturbed him, and in the morning there remained a residue of the night's unease.

He felt ordinary, but knew that the very fact of realizing his ordinariness made him extraordinary. "Father," returned Joe, "I know what I say and mean—well, better than you do when you hear me."

But I reflected that surely I had always known him to be a performer, even if the mechanics of the performance had been invisible to me. It is *bewitching*. Aloud, I said: "The unforeseen is what is beautiful."

What I needed in the end was just to love the child. How I

long to surrender!

"How did that damned thing get in here?" he asks.

His mother is there. I couldn't have dressed her up better myself.

"Poor dear, you wouldn't notice, but I've been away." She stared at him pensively as he exhorted her, pleaded, warned her.

"Don't kiss me so hard, mother." His voice had an edge of annoyance that no longer surprised me. A sadist. We were terrified of Joe—and yet we adored him. And suddenly he realized she was crying. He was obviously alarmed. "I don't like to kiss people." Joe felt there was no way for him to be completely open with his parents without upsetting them.

Our night had started as such a good night. That time is gone: gone forever.

"Oh, what the hell's the difference where I am?" Is this a genuine question or the beginning of a speech? She powdered her face. "I have seen enough Americans in America," she said, "and enough English in England, and I do not believe that the Italians will take much interest in me." There she stood, trying to soothe herself with the scent of flowers and the fading, beautiful evening. On the other hand, she is fiercely sexual, quite unashamed and untouched by coyness. "Darling, I'm leaving for San Francisco this evening and will be gone six weeks. I feel kind of silly sitting still to read about someone else's adventures when I could be having my own."

He held out his hand. For hours they sat together, or walked in the dark, and talked only a few, almost meaningless words.

Up and down the quiet streets under the new moon went the woman and the boy.

The Joe she knew receded, faded, became lost.

She refuses to see things clearly that can only be seen darkly.

Whatever else is unsure in this stinking dunghill of a world a mother's love is not.

ℰ 37 ℭ

The remainder of that same afternoon I spent at the town's hairdressing salon, where my hair was trimmed and my nails finely manicured by an obsequious little fusspot of a man who, with his own elaborately crimped and wavy locks, was the very image of a barber in a French farce; in the more expensive of its two men's shops in search of a 'stylish' silk tie that might set off to advantage the pale grey, slim-waisted suit I had not yet worn in Chesterfield as it had been bought and set aside for exactly the present occasion; then in a chic and overwhelmingly fragrant flower shop— located, possibly as a result of someone's drolly irreverent sense of cause and effect, next door to the gun store—where I purchased a vast bouquet of white 'long-stemmed' roses.

I watched David to see what he thought of it, and he had not yet made up his mind. Oozing apple pie pessimism. In this large sense, criticism is, as T.S. Eliot observed, "as inevitable as breathing."

But could I find my way back to the way I was before this all began?

There was a pause—just long enough for an angel to pass, flying slowly.

That night I had some dreadful dreams.

ಬ 38 ಛ

Roy was in a panic. He said very distinctly, and looking at the carpet, "She's gone." He was in love; it did not follow that he was loved, or ever would be. He had *barricaded* himself in his house. He told me his despair was from being misunderstood. As is known, however, a man too carried away by passion, especially if he is of a certain age, becomes completely blind and is ready to suspect hope where there is no hope at all; moreover, he takes leave of his senses and acts like a foolish child, though he be of the most palatial mind. Love is the most profound aesthetic experience in a person's life. On that note, he took the cap off a bottle of beer. "Gimme a cigarette." He was ugly, lively, and filled with the spirit of libertinism. There is nothing, he thought, nothing so blissful in the world as falling back into the arms of a woman who is—possibly bad for you. At least he was happy for a time. "I was once a man," he said, "but now I'm not."

During the period in my life when I was most *unhappy*, I used to frequent—for reasons hard to justify, and without a trace of sexual attraction—a woman whom I only found appealing because of her ridiculous appearance: as though my lot required in these circumstances a bird of ill omen to keep me company.

"I think this room is the saddest place I have ever been." How could anyone live for long in such a place? "Wake up and smell the espresso." Two or three books had been placed on each shelf, for decoration—exactly what bad designers do to provide their clients with a bogus cultural pedigree while leaving space for Lalique vases, African fetishes, silver plates, and crystal decanters. "Let me guess who decorated this room."

Sometimes staying in the house can be bad.

"I don't believe you," Roy said. I could hear her talking to herself. She did not know what she thought. The alert host at an opportunity lifted his glass to Humanity and, when the toast had been drunk, he threw open a window significantly. "Is there anything here you'd like to put on?" he asked. "If you would step with me for a moment into the bathroom . . . I'll be brief," he said.

It's creepy, the language of police.

"I am a camera," I said. "I'm doing a nonfiction novel." Art, on this view of things, does not result from work. The artist, like the God of the creation, remains within or behind or beyond or above his handiwork, invisible, refined out of existence, indifferent, paring his fingernails.

Excitement is muddling my thoughts, my face is blazing with heat.

"You'll succeed at whatever you're passionate about. But isn't it dangerous for a girl your age?" Seated, she opened her handbag and used the mirror to look at her teeth. Next he showed some anxiety about the adjective "handsome." It was difficult to argue with a man whose knowledge of the early recordings of Connie Francis was practically flawless. By now it was darker in the low-arched room than it was outside. "They never have my size," he said breathlessly, "and I refuse to tell them it's for a friend." Frustration had been puckering his spirit. As the evening wore on I began to suspect that I was in the presence of a desperate man. Her mean, hunted look was driving me insane. His waking hours were spent in a prison of rituals and superstitions, his "mania," as he called it. I don't know how he made his decisions in those days. We believe in ourselves, as we do not believe in others.

An hour goes so slowly when someone is talking.

The rest of the day was spent devouring a book by Havelock Ellis.

That night, I wrestled with myself for hours and hours.

ಬಿ 39 ೞ

I am teaching myself perfect freedom. So far, so good. More or less meaningless. I spent twenty-four hours in reflections, all of which ended by convincing me of my mistakes and making me despise myself. I didn't understand a thing. Is this the so-called "blue hour"? I was so depressed that, unable to talk about my torment with anyone, I continuously brooded. Played the piano. "You can either resent the way life is ordained, or be intrigued by it," wrote the critic Denis Donoghue. I remembered that the Hindus—or was it the Buddhists?—taught that a man should lead an ordinary life as a merchant and a father but that as old age approached he should become a monk and meditate and fast and give up the world and even his family and sex. You had your period of civic business, then you withdrew to discover what life was really about and to begin the long process of preparing for death.

I ruminated for perhaps six seconds on the words "get used to" and felt a kind of very slight melancholy that can be expressed only by the image of a pile of sand or rubbish.

Obediently the body levers itself out of bed—wincing from twinges in the arthritic thumbs and the left knee, mildly nauseated by the pylorus in a state of spasm—and shambles naked into the bathroom, where its bladder is emptied and it is weighed: still a bit over 150 pounds, in spite of all that toiling at the gym!

I owe my salvation only to chance.

That night there was a snowfall. White streets, white roofs, all sounds softened. As I walked up the rue de la Chausée-d'Antin, swimming on waves of sadness and grief and thinking about death, I raised my head and saw a huge stone angel, dark as night, looming up at the end of the street.

Yes, I am dreaming aloud. 'Tis very strange.

Homosexuality does not stem from any dirty little secret. Nothing is abnormal about it except its price. Yes, but what is it? To whom could I put this question (with any hope of an answer)? It is when I am masculine that I want to make love to a man. Repression is a cat without a smile in the heterosexual streets, and a smile without a cat in homosexual minds. One ages quickly enough without such complications. There is a proportion of humans, oscillating between fifty and a hundred percent, that carries the desire for the same sex.

This morning, more snow, and *lieder* broadcast on the radio.

Parenthood, it seems, makes you nervous for the rest of your life.

Across the sky, like a cornea filling with blood, came a fearful darkening.

∞ 40 ∞

The inquest concluded that Roy had died of unknown causes, a verdict to which I added the words, in the deep and dark hours of the night.

෨ 41 ෬

I got there at three, dressed in black. They were waiting for me, looking expensive; svelte and composed. The house was full of the silence of snow. I urinated, emitted gas.

David's face assumed an expression of horror. "Put me to the test, I accept it!" cried David.

Does he think he's in *West Side Story* or something? It was one of the traits that endeared him to me. "But, David, you must insist on a proper rehearsal." He got drunk every day, I no longer knew what to do with him. He would never be popular: he saw that. "I am a fool with a heart but no brains, and you are a fool with brains but no heart; and we're both unhappy, and we both suffer. You must yield to my ardor without resisting me in the slightest, and be sure that I will respect your innocence."

"Oh, damn," said David very softly. "--Suck it yourself, sugarstick!"

Sometimes when I'm at work I find myself drifting off, thinking of the low light by which we dine, how he's taken to keeping a bottle of my preferred bourbon in the house. But he must also accept the responsibility which goes with my gratitude.

He himself repeatedly said that—except for poetry—love was the only thing that absorbed his interest. Our entire reasoning comes down to surrendering to feeling.

At all events, his somber mood does not appear to have lifted.

❧ 42 ❧

Joe was taking the offensive. "Say that I am asleep and tell her to go away. She depresses me." He knew that her love for him would drown him, that he could not live with such a passion, with the sense of being always emotionally outclassed.

"Certainly not, it would be impolite. What were you doing—praying? Are you allowed to do that? Why would someone go on doing such things?"

"Why not," he said rather stupidly.

"What are you thinking, boy?"

"Goddam if *I* know," he said, his inflection implying that the answer to that question was hopelessly obscure. "It is a way of connecting with something larger than oneself and, indeed, larger than any self. I should like to see the mystery of being. I can't find myself a second father."

Exactly.

I like it when he calls me daddy. And yet the victory is not absolute. One who thinks he is a good father is not a good father; one who thinks he is a good husband is not a good husband. I never was very good at getting away with anything.

"What say you, Eleanor? And where have you been—if it isn't indiscreet . . . ?"

She wore a blue dress and a white sailor hat. She did not know what to say, or how to express herself more genuinely. She dealt with moral problems as a cleaver deals with meat: and in this case she had made up her mind. She reminded me of my mother, her infinite patience and the way she looked like a weeping saint asking to be slapped in the face. I can see her standing at the kitchen sink scraping carrots. She stands on the porch of her fabulous New England inn with her artificial dessert topping, made from lard, engine oil, preservatives extracted from offal and animal screams. History takes a certain course, and it *adds up* to New England. She highly disapproves of my deficiency (in household matters) and my (pathological) irresponsibility when it comes to heavy lifting, tidying up, cleaning and other domestic divertimenti, which, I admit, I hold in utter contempt.

It began to rain over the woods outside, and a mood of depression and of unspeakable loneliness suddenly felled me like a hammer-stroke. Soon I will be forty-four years old. Writing a book is a horrible, exhausting struggle, like a long bout of some painful illness.

I have not a desire but a need for solitude.

How often we need to be assured of what we know in the old ways of knowing—how seldom we can afford to venture beyond the pale into that chromatic fantasy where, as Rilke said (in 1908!), "begins the revision of categories, where something past comes again, as though out of the future; something formerly accomplished as something to be completed." I love the old questions. But if the acutest sage be often at his wits' ends to understand living character, shall those who are not sages expect to run and read character in those mere phantoms which flit along a page, like shadows along a wall? But I will not philosophize.

I would like to be a gigolo offering myself to all. (Wilde speaks of his "curious mixture of ardor and of indifference . . . I would go to the stake for a sensation and be a sceptic to the last.")

ॐ 43 ☙

David and I had a tremendous adventure. We had been to Chartres and were on our way back to Paris. (Talking, talking.) It seemed that the ride would never end.

"This traffic jam has a permanent look about it."

Outside, the land stretches, empty, to the horizon; the sky opens, with speeding clouds.

"What seems beautiful to me, what I should like to write, is a book about nothing."

❧ 44 ☙

Something lovely happened last night. There was zest in the air and a sweet sadness like a hovering ghost. A policeman entered the courtyard and asked what was going on. With a stick in his hand, he kept vigil in the chicken coop until dawn, frightening away a skunk by barking like a dog. Here he drank several glasses of beer in rapid succession, and when he came out it was night. "Are you trying to get inside me?" he asked. "I came here to find myself," he said as he walked from the front door of my apartment to the elevator across the hall, "but instead, I got lost." He bowed and retired, a verse or two already beginning to creep into his head.

And that was it. And then there was nothing.

෴ 45 ೞ

Silence is a prophecy, one which the artist's actions can be understood as attempting both to fulfill and to reverse.

I have a prophecy of my own: that soon the day will come when man shall bitterly repent having neglected, scorned, or renounced his duty to spread, wherever he might, the simple light of unbelief.

❧ 46 ☙

I am writing this book near a monastery that stands deep in the woods, among rocks and thorns. And I'm still anxious. Always alone. This is a life of eternal longing. I move books from one place to another, myself as well, / I don't know what to do with all of this. Our solutions are redescriptions of our problems. Man has become a counter-natural animal, and we have called that process the appearance of intelligence.

How did we come to these corrupted times? As the activity of the mystic must end in a *via negativa*, a theology of God's absence, a craving for the cloud of unknowing beyond knowledge and for the silence beyond speech, so art must tend toward anti-art, the elimination of the "subject" (the "object," the "image"), the substitution of chance for intention, and the pursuit of silence.

This is, as we have seen, an epic situation; but it is also an "Orphic" situation: not because Orpheus "sings," but because the writer and Orpheus are both under the same prohibition, which constitutes their "song": the prohibition from turning back toward what they love.

The only good thing about childhood is that no one really remembers it, or rather, that's the only thing about it to like: this forgetting. It is endless.

Forget it; forget it.

Zee End.

❧ The Books ☙

The following pages contain all of the quotes, in order of appearance, that make up *An Honest Ghost*. Each quote is followed by the author who wrote it; the book in Rick Whitaker's library from which the sentence was taken; and the page number on which it appears in that edition.

An Honest Ghost: William Shakespeare *Hamlet* Act 1, Scene 5
Happiness is an: Thomas Szasz *The Second Sin* 36

❧ 1 ☙

I am unpacking: Walter Benjamin *Illuminations* 59
I have been: Andre Gide *The Counterfeiters* 180
It is growing: Hart Crane *Library of America: Complete Poems and Selected Letters* 358
There are limits: Rob Stephenson *Passes Through* 26
Life lived by: Susan Sontag *I, etcetera: Stories* 15
You go back: Samuel Beckett *Nohow On* 46
The subjective universe: Ludwig Wittgenstein *Notebooks 1914-1916* 41
There was an: Teju Cole *Open City* 166
It seemed neither: Carl Van Vechten *Parties* 105
"How can you: Max Ewing *Going Somewhere* 47
He was twenty-four: Max Ewing *Going Somewhere* 22
At the moment: Adam Thirwell *Delighted States* 38

David said, "I: Don DeLillo *The Names* 260
My splendid David: J. M. Barrie *The White Bird* 274
My daily recreational: Charles Kaiser *The Gay Metropolis* 243
"What color were: Don DeLillo *The Names* 108
Our little love: Alfred Chester *Looking for Genet* 161
"Oh! How long: Andre Gide *The Counterfeiters* 165
Well!: Jacques Lacan *Four Fundamental Concepts of Psychoanalysis* 109
I was dealing: Glen Baxter *Returns to Normal* (no page numbers)
He was really: David Wojnarowicz *Memories That Smell Like Gasoline* 39
I wrote in: Benjamin Sonnenberg *Lost Property* 93
There was something: D. H. Lawrence *Sons and Lovers* 99
To be in: Anita Brookner *Look at Me* 92
Sometimes he purred: Lincoln Kirstein *By With To and From* 37
He often pretended: Ben Marcus *Notable American Women* 130
The action signaled: Elizabeth Hardwick *Sleepless Nights* 15
I could spare: Thomas Bernhard "The Joiner", *German Short Stories* (Ed. David Constantine) 271
I would lie: Virginia Woolf *Orlando* 90
I have never: Graham Greene *Travels with My Aunt* 3
A few years: Albert Camus *The Fall* 17
I lived in: Theophile Gautier *Mademoiselle de Maupin* 144
It was very: W. Somerset Maugham *The Razor's Edge* 187
These arrangements turned: Edmund White *Nocturnes for the King of Naples* 2
Few men have: Charles Baudelaire *The Mirror of Art* 192
Occasionally I had: Robert Bolaño *By Night in Chile* 85
David frowned: Eleanor Porter *Just David* 202
He was not: John Banville *Doctor Copernicus* 123
It had been: Brenda McCreight *Parenting Your Adopted Older Child* 187
When his friends: Robert Bolaño *Amulet* 79
His irony, intended: Susan Sontag *I, etcetera.: Stories* 48

Rick Whitaker

Prodded by his: Nathanael West *Miss Lonelyhearts* 39
Once when I: Richard Gilman *Common and Uncommon Mass* 49
His rage had: John Banville *Doctor Copernicus* 78
The most innocent-seeming: John Banville *Doctor Copernicus* 112
Cops always questioned: Alfred Chester *The Exquisite Corpse* 27
His early childhood: James Schuyler *Alfred and Guinivere* viii
     (introduction by John Ashbery)
He was a: Rick Whitaker *Assuming the Position* 128
He died of: Alex Ross *Listen to This* 8
He lived a: Gilbert Highet *Poets in a Landscape* 174
Shall I describe: Neil Bartlett *Ready to Catch Him Should He Fall* 240
I found it: Theophile Gautier *Mademoiselle de Maupin* 317
His mother had: Don DeLillo *The Names* 225
After one first: Max Ewing *Going Somewhere* 51
She attended to: Max Ewing *Going Somewhere* 50
The immense accretion: Susan Howe *My Emily Dickinson* 105
She could be: Lydie Salvayre *The Power of Flies* 1
She drank, she: Elizabeth Hardwick *Sleepless Nights* 19
Her clothes seemed: Victoria Redel *The Border of Truth* 39
She had a: Djuna Barnes *Nightwood* 84
Her family, her: Willa Cather *Youth and the Bright Medusa* 85
David admires her: J. M. Barrie *The White Bird* 132
How tender people: Maximilien Robespierre *Virtue and Terror* 28
"I'm rough and: Rudy Wilson *The Red Truck* 140
One often makes: Ludwig Wittgenstein *Notebooks 1914-1916* 42
"What a sweet: Nathanael West *Miss Lonelyhearts* 29
Her voice was: Nathanael West *Miss Lonelyhearts* 49
I will not: Jane Gardam *The Flight of the Maidens* 211
David leaned my: Don DeLillo *The Names* 131
He was stretched: Colette *The Pure and the Impure* 44
He puts on: Ludwig Wittgenstein *Lectures on Philosophical
     Psychology* 1946-47 63

138.

If there is: Samuel Beckett *Disjecta* 65
Though he was: Voltaire *Zadig* 21
Even more commendable: Voltaire *Zadig* 21
Very quickly, he: James Blake *The Joint* 183
He talked incessantly: Virginia Woolf *Orlando* 91
He was adequately: Andre Gide *The Counterfeiters* 205
Flushed with his: F. Scott Fitzgerald *The Great Gatsby* 137
I've been told: Montaigne *Selected Essays* 15
David recalled dimly: Andre Gide *The Counterfeiters* 205
Not that there: Edmund White *City Boy* 80
That is how: John Banville *The Infinities* 7
He spent his: Alan Bennett *Writing Home* 570
A bell beat: James Joyce *Portrait of the Artist as a Young Man* 191
Although none of: Susan Sontag *I, etcetera: Stories* 15
I am interested: Susan Sontag *I, etcetera: Stories* 72
But it could: Joseph Breuer and Sigmund Freud *Studies in
    Hysteria* 189
Some of my: Robert Frost *The Notebooks of Robert Frost* 299
It is impossible: David Lehman, ed. *Great American Prose Poems* 221
Today is not: Gioia Timpanelli *Sometimes the Soul* 14
I swear I: Elizabeth Bishop *One Art* 529
But what kind: Adam Phillips *Going Sane* 17
We long for: Robert Lowell *Collected Prose* 192
Life and death: Gertrude Stein *Wars I Have Seen* 121
I believe in: Noel Coward *Lyrics* 73
My life is: David Lehman, ed. *Great American Prose Poems* 146
 I live in: Susan Howe *My Emily Dickinson* 38
(Like Holden Caulfield: James Blake *The Joint* 234
All of us: W. G. Sebald *Austerlitz* 71
The Zen masters: Daisetz T. Suzuki *Zen and Japanese Culture* 7
All work is: David Lehman, ed. *Great American Prose Poems* 112
Shall we make: Maximilien Robespierre *Virtue and Terror* 115

Rick Whitaker

The story that: Danilo Kiš *A Tomb for Boris* 1
To say that: Jorge Luis Borges *Collected Fictions* 480
This is my: Christopher Priest *The Glamour* 2
Not my usual: David McConnell *The Firebrat* 3

ℬ 2 ℭ

Day before yesterday: Elizabeth Bishop *One Art* 336
I got drunk: Paul Klee *The Diaries of Paul Klee* 186
I wasn't good: August Kleinzahler *Cutty One Rock* 80
That was about: Jean Echenoz *I'm Gone* 12
Soon I'd be: Edmund White *My Lives* 221
I took a: Charles Henri Ford *Like Water From a Bucket* 198
A black man: Virginia Woolf *Orlando* 56
The world to: Thomas Bernhard *Prose* 127
A part of: Glenway Wescott *Continual Lessons* 318
I didn't want: David McConnell *Firebrat* 2
I was amazed: Shohaku Okumura *Living By Vow* 133
I was lost: Dante trans. Mary Jo Bang *The Inferno* 15
Loneliness rose to: George W. S. Trow *In the Context of No Context* 49
When I got: Alfred Chester *Looking for Genet* 162
A sound of: Robert Bolaño *Amulet* 27
Who comes here: Jacques Lacan *Four Fundamental Concepts of Psychoanalysis* 113
Sometimes a venturesome: Mark Merlis *American Studies* 59
(O the weakness: Maximilien Robespierre *Virtue and Terror* 104
Still, the only: Mark Merlis *American Studies* 57
Ding-dong: Richard Rodriguez *Brown* 51
A minute later: Nathanael West *Miss Lonelyhearts* 139
I blushed intensely: Robert Bolaño *By Night in Chile* 14
Moving, as I: Fran Lebowitz *Reader* 137

140.

The child was: Djuna Barnes *Nightwood* 68

We shook hands: Gore Vidal *Palimpsest* 122

He seemed bloodless: Paula Fox *Poor George* 18

I was all: Rob Stephenson *Passes Through* 27

Silence: Theodore Dreiser *An American Tragedy* 7

The uncertainty lasted: Danilo Kiš *A Tomb for Boris* 11

I would not: Darcy O'Brien *A Way of Life, Like Any Other* 5

There are only: Jean Genet *The Declared Enemy* 10

A shiver ran: Robert Bolaño *By Night in Chile* 84

It was a: Vladimir Nabokov *Laughter in the Dark* 21

He looked extremely: James Baldwin *Notes of a Native Son* 157

"Joe, how are: Charles Dickens *Great Expectations* 255

The visitor glided: Aidan Higgins *Notes from a Receding Past* 146

He gives me: Anne Landsman *The Rowing Lesson* 177

"I haf someding: Darcy O'Brien *A Way of Life, Like Any Other* 23

He looked at: Fyodor Dostoevsky *The House of the Dead* 230

"Please answer me: Albert Camus *The Plague* 50

How can I: Theophile Gautier *Mademoiselle de Maupin* 134

The question was: Sylvia Townsend Warner *Summer Will Show* 122

I do not: Diane Williams *It Was Like My Trying to Have a Tender-Hearted Nature* 85

I don't want: Ivy Compton-Burnett *Darkness and Day* 7

Absolute silence: Darcy O'Brien *A Way of Life, Like Any Other* 49

"And besides, don't: Evan S. Connell *Mrs. Bridge* 122

This is a: Denis Donoghue *American Classics* 238

"Well well well: Anthony Burgess *A Clockwork Orange* 147

Unconditional surrender: Gertrude Stein *Wars I Have Seen* 110

Is that right: Mary McCarthy *The Group* 310

"You bet!" Joe: Ken Kesey *Sometimes a Great Notion* 492

"No harm in: F. Scott Fitzgerald *The Great Gatsby* 60

"I guess some: David McConnell *The Silver Hearted* 125

He noticed then: Kenzaburo Oe *A Personal Matter* 86

Rick Whitaker

"Don't worry," I: Geoff Dyer *Out of Sheer Rage: Wrestling with D. H. Lawrence* 26

"Daddy was talking: Noel Coward *Pomp and Circumstance* 86

"Your father is: Darcy O'Brien *A Way of Life, Like Any Other* 24

This was all: Kenzaburo Oe *A Quiet Life* 3

"I am the: Italo Calvino *Invisible Cities* 152

"I like your: Plato *Collected Dialogues* 587

"De bargain it: Darcy O'Brien *A Way of Life, Like Any Other* 25

It was the: Giacomo Casanova *History of My Life* 932

One is always: James Lasdun *The Horned Man* 125

All was greyness: W. G. Sebald *After Nature* 65

"I haven't figured: Binnie Kirshenbaum *Pure Poetry* 50

"But you really: Dezso Kosztalanyi *Skylark* 76

And so we: James Danziger *American Photographs* (introduction, no page numbers)

Phew: James Joyce *Finnegans Wake* 522

That night, after: Kenzaburo Oe *A Quiet Life* 125

The twilight desert: Kenzaburo Oe *A Quiet Life* 127

What does this: Daniel Dennett *Consciousness Explained* 130

The rain beat: Anton Chekhov *The Portable Chekhov* 384

All night long: Philip Roth *Professor of Desire* 262

The dream is: Bruce Duffy *The World As I Found It* 31

The lamp is: Samuel Beckett *Disjecta* 22

℘ 3 ℘

But whirligig Time: Richard Rodriguez *Brown* 143

I awoke, yet: John Ashbery *Flow Chart* 192

Lost in darkness: David Lynch *Lost Highway* xi

Living with a: Chris Kutschera *The Kurdish National Movement* 94

The first three: Amy Hempel *At the Gates of the Animal Kingdom* 43

142.

My artistic nature: Lydie Salvayre *Portrait of the Artist as a Domesticated Animal* 23
It was my: Andrew Holleran *Nights in Aruba* 31
Suspense is fascinating: Nick Piombino *Contradicta* 20
It is fear: Montaigne *Selected Essays* 25
I regret sometimes: Guy Hocquenghem *Screwball Asses* 16
The taboo gives: Adam Phillips *Equals* 58
But most men: Alan Bennett *Writing Home* 64
Fear tweaks the: Christopher Isherwood *A Single Man* 9
So David tells: J. M. Barrie *The White Bird* 11
Naturally: Merle Miller *On Being Different* 16
Though blue, the: Albert Camus *The Plague* 36
Very strange: David Lynch *Lost Highway* 17
To look at: Susan Sontag *Styles of Radical Will* 10

ᘓ 4 ᘔ

"I suppose my: Ivy Compton-Burnett *Parents and Children* 7
"I know you: Andre Tellier *Twilight Men* 72
From the first: Thomas Bernhard *The Loser* 10
"I wonder why: Ivy Compton-Burnett *Parents and Children* 17
Few emotions are: W. G. Sebald *On the Natural History of Destruction* 129
She sounded slightly: Colm Toibin *The Master* 252
Her voice softened: Heinrich Boll *The Silent Angel* 139
She was capable: Wendy Moffat *A Great Unrecorded History* 7
"Oh, well-behaved: Georges Bataille *The Blue of Noon* 18
A hard-bitten: Virginia Woolf *Orlando* 40
She's insane and: Mary Jo Bang *Inferno* 18
At this very: Kazuo Ishiguro *The Remains of the Day* 48
Poor Eleanor, how: Edward St Aubyn *At Last* 104

Rick Whitaker

When we reflect: Shunryu Suzuki *Zen Mind, Beginner's Mind* 39

In a flurry: Susanna Pinney, ed. *I'll Stand by You: Letters of Sylvia Townsend Warner* 13

Her beauty seemed: Andrew Holleran *Nights In Aruba* 34

"In this heat,": Ronald Firbank *Three More Novels* 55

She was on: W. Somerset Maugham *The Razor's Edge* 212

It was a: Sylvia Townsend Warner *Summer Will Show* 85

New York on: Anita Brookner *Look at Me* 41

There all the: James Joyce *Ulysses* 37

She was silent: Jenny McPhee *A Man of No Moon* 268

Her unassailable assumption: Jane Gardam *Faith Fox* 63

She often refers: Peter Cameron *Someday This Pain Will Be Useful To You* 57

But her beauty: Bill Pronzini *The Hidden* 41

Her feelings came: *NOON* 2007 ed., Diane Williams 160

She stressed her: Denton Welch *Maiden Voyage* 257

Naturally she is: Gertrude Stein *Wars I Have Seen* 146

"David," she said: Honoré de Balzac *Lost Illusions* 505

Bravo!: Lydie Salvayre *Portrait of the Artist as a Domesticated Animal* 179

She stood there: H. Rider Haggard *She* 161

I am but: H. Rider Haggard *She* 187

In any case: Gore Vidal *Palimpsest* 159

Anxiety like a: Leo Lerman *The Grand Surprise* 511

Anxiety being the: David Markson *Wittgenstein's Mistress* 72

I expected sympathy: Gore Vidal *Palimpsest* 239

ৎ৹ 5 ೲ

The weather had: Joris-Karl Huysmans *Against Nature* 166

It was hot: Theodore Dreiser *An American Tragedy* 514

I spent that: James Lasdun *The Horned Man* 161

I was lying: Noel Coward *Pomp and Circumstance* 75

I read it: Shohaku Okumura *Living By Vow* 133

The only fact: Denis Donoghue *American Classics* 205

I like to: David Lehman, ed. *Great American Prose Poems* 216

There is no: Italo Calvino *Invisible Cities* 48

Above me, in: H. G. Wells *The Time Machine* 118

Here we are: Celine *Death on the Installment Plan* 15

Take a few: B. K. S. Iyengar *Light on Yoga* 22

I felt naked: H. G. Wells *The Time Machine* 27

So I enter: B. K. S. Lyengar *Light on Yoga* 394

In many respects: Tim Dean *Unlimited Intimacy* 195

What stumps me: Lucia Perillo *I've Heard the Vultures Singing* 18

Everything was becoming: Georges Bataille *The Blue of Noon* 84

I kept having: Gordon Lish *Zimzum* 75

Why do we: Slavoj Zizek *Did Somebody Say Totalitarianism?* 196

I used to: Robert Bolaño *By Night in Chile* 1

But gay men: Edmund White *City Boy* 80

We always worry: Michael Cunningham *By Nightfall* 53

I am almost: Ludwig Wittgenstein *Notebooks 1914-1916* 31

The razor-sharp: Robert Bolaño *Amulet* 49

ഏ 6 ങ

My decision to: Gore Vidal *Palimpsest* 385

I lacked both: Alex Ross *Listen to This* 7

I am forty: Kenneth Koch *1000 Avant-Garde Plays* 19

Beneath everything else: Edmund White *Nocturnes for the King of Naples* 88

The place was: Graham Greene *The Heart of the Matter* 8

The problem is: Iannis Xenakis *Formalized Music* 29

Rick Whitaker

I opened the: Teju Cole *Open City* 164
Generally, even then: David Markson *Wittgenstein's Mistress* 240
A lost soul: Robert Frost *The Notebooks of Robert Frost* 373
That's me: Sherrie Eldridge *20 Things Adopted Kids Wish Their Adoptive Parents Knew* 169
The psychological feeling: Theodor Adorno *The Stars Down to Earth* 128
I dropped David: J. M. Barrie *The White Bird* 211
"Did you know: H. Rider Haggard *She* 81
Several times he: Colm Toibin *The Master* 248
David extended his: Carl Van Vechten *Parties* 173
"I'm so sorry: Edith Wharton *The Age of Innocence* 62
The things one: David Markson *Wittgenstein's Mistress* 53
"I am glad: Noel Coward *Pomp and Circumstance* 12
The irony of: Charles Kaiser *1968 in America* 239
"How are you: Alfred Chester *The Exquisite Corpse* 49
He does not: Giacomo Casanova *History of My Life* 931
"I am the: Andre Tellier *Twilight Men* 24
There was a: Walter Kirn *My Hard Bargain* 69
But soon this: Huysmans *Against Nature* 207
What, if anything: Harold Bloom *Hamlet: Poem Unlimited* 86
What was the: H. Rider *Haggard She* 96
Who will speak: Michael Cunningham *By Nightfall* 54
"Which cathedral do: Denton Welch *Maiden Voyage* 37
A moan burst: Carl Van Vechten *Parties* 130
He was handsome: Henry James *The Aspern Papers and The Turn of the Screw* 149
His broad shoulders: Edmund White *My Lives* 222
"But you have: John Ashbery *April Galleons* 24
You are too: Gore Vidal *Two Sisters* 14
It's too serious: Edith Wharton *The Age of Innocence* 105
Amused, I nodded: Colette *Pure and Impure* 15

"I may be: Rachel Ingalls *Mrs. Caliban* 7
We will see: Frederick Seidel *Poems 1959-2009* 186
"Fortunately, I know: J. D. Salinger *Franny and Zooey* 157
"I'm interested in: David McConnell *The Silver Hearted* 122
"Ah.": David McConnell *The Silver Hearted* 123
His leisure hours: Alex Ross *Listen to This* 126
There is, of: Michael Cunningham *By Nightfall* 19
He was young: Virginia Woolf *Orlando* 28
And so on: Roland Barthes *Reader* xiii
He was a: James Joyce *Portait of the Artist as a Young Man* 192
Take care of: Susanna Pinney, ed. *I'll Stand by You: Letters of
    Sylvia Townsend Warner* 19
Do you love: Kenneth Koch *1000 Avant-Garde Plays* 19

ℰ 7 ℭ

The cuckoo came: John Ashbery and James Schuyler *A Nest of
    Ninnies* 40
It was a: James Joyce *Dubliners* 31
Summer was a: Rudy Wilson *The Red Truck* 129
Inwardness, calm, solitude: Roland Barthes *Mourning Diary* 100
No, that's too: Merle Miller *On Being Different* 19
Silence: Vladimir Nabokov *Laughter in the Dark* 192
At one point: Ron Padgett *Joe* 24
I must photograph: Charles Henri Ford *Like Water from a Bucket* 153
Little ineffectual unquenchable: E.M. Forster *A Passage to India* 120
It was the: Virginia Woolf *Orlando* 85
He was looking: Thomas Bernhard "The Joiner" *German Short
    Stories* ed., David Constantine 263
He is not: John Banville *The Infinities* 9
Solitude had acted: J-K. Huysmans *Against Nature* 84

At school, he: Edgar Saltus *Mr. Incoul's Misadventure* 4
The other children: Edmund White *Genet* xv
In the meantime: Thomas Bernhard *The Loser* 16
There was an: David Wojnarowicz *Memories That Smell Like Gasoline* 27
He's a beautiful: James Blake *The Joint* 167
It hurts to: John Waters *Role Models* 294
I have often: Gore Vidal *Palimpsest* 295
I admit I: Edmund White *Genet* 100
(In Wilde's phrase: Roland Barthes *Reader* xvi
Similarly, I sometimes: David Levithan *The Full Spectrum* 172
We can only: Ivy Compton-Burnett *Darkness and Day* 8

⁎ 8 ⁏

By Thanksgiving, Joe: Ron Padgett *Joe* 87
He stayed at: Filip Noterdaeme *The Autobiography of Daniel J. Isengart* 73
He asked me: James Blake *The Joint* 167
"Even if there: Kenzaburo Oe *A Quiet Life* 149
I don't want: Sam Massey *Return of the Greek* 47
I am like: Conor Cruise O'Brien *Camus* 29
We're going to: Giacomo Leopardi *Canti* 25
Salvation lies in: Sarah Bakewell *How to Live* 35
"Can't you smell: J-K Huysmans *Against Nature* 118
"What is it?: Brenda McCreight *Parenting Your Adopted Older Child* 32
I suddenly thought: Frederick Seidel *Poems 1959-2009* 3
He was the: D. H. Lawrence *Sons and Lovers* 85
What had been: Gioia Timpanelli *Sometimes the Soul* 21
It was like: Franz Kafka *The Castle* 27

"Yes, yes, I: Graham Greene *The Heart of the Matter* 31
I feel in: D. H. Lawrence *Selected Letters* 260
You must have: Max Ewing *Going Somewhere* 79
You're not angry: O. Henry *The Four Million* 67
"No," said Joe: Charles Dickens *Barnaby Rudge* 105
I want his: James Joyce *Ulysses* 46
"I think that: Sam Massey *Return of the Greek* 65
Anyway, you'll get: Mark Merlis *American Studies* 168
"Will you?" said: Charles Dickens *Barnaby Rudge* 584
"What is that: John Banville *The Infinities* 11
"Men are such: Michael Cunningham *By Nightfall* 53
Score one for: Michael Cunningham *By Nightfall* 55
The world was: Vladimir Nabokov *Laughter in the Dark* 192
The nature of: Andrezj Walicki *A History of Russian Thought* 24
But in all: James Blake *The Joint* 313
I get bored: Umberto Eco *The Mysterious Flame of Queen Loana* 327
This is the: Alan Bennett *Writing Home* xiii
To me there: Ivy Compton-Burnett *Darkness and Day* 14
In the course: J-K Huysmans *Against Nature* 118
But the city: Gilbert Highet *Poets in a Landscape* 162
"We are both: Charles Henri Ford *Like Water From a Bucket* 214
He was no: Edmund White *Rimbaud* 35
"You're probably wondering: Plato *Gorgias* 12
He begins to: Giles and Miller, eds. *The Arts of Contemplative Care* 75
Joe looked at: Charles Dickens *Great Expectations* 559
Every heartstring is: Edmund White *Rimbaud* 21
It would be: W. H. Auden *Forewords and Afterwords* 292
It took him: Rudyard Kipling *Kim* 118
The eloquence of: Dickens *Barnaby Rudge* 632
The silence speaks: James Joyce *Finnegans Wake* 10
Like a big: Kenzaburo Oe *A Quiet Life* 2
He knew I: Lincoln Kirstein *By With To and From* 70

Rick Whitaker

Thank God for: Frederick Seidel *Poems 1959-2009* 5
You can count: Sherrie Eldridge *20 Things Adopted Kids Wish Their Adoptive Parents Knew* 143
Everybody knows you: John Waters *Role Models* 264
"I'm the man: D. H. Lawrence *Sons and Lovers* 84
He knocked at: Charles Kaiser *The Gay Metropolis* 21
"I am!": Charles Dickens *Great Expectations* 164
But many questions: *Hungarian Photographs* 26
Either way, I: George W. S. Trow *Bullies* 4

ଘ 9 ଓ

David watched my: J. M. Barrie *The White Bird* 101
"You hear what: Charles Dickens *Barnaby Rudge* 10
We must be: Charles Dickens *Barnaby Rudge* 109
You're so reluctant: Peter Cameron *Someday This Pain Will Be Useful To You* 55
Am I upsetting: J. D. Salinger *Franny and Zooey* 196
He looked over: Sarah Schulman *The Child* 19
"Oh, you'll see: E. F. Benson *David Blaize* 54
Here he poured: Virginia Woolf *Orlando* 89
Joe could only: Charles Dickens *Barnbaby Rudge* 633
"You're useless: Binnie Kirshenbaum *Pure Poetry* 55
He told him: Danilo Kiš *A Tomb for Boris* 12
"It's not my: Thomas Bernhard *The Loser* 14
Don't we all: Jean-Christophe Valtat *03* 68
We identify with: Tim Dean *Unlimited Intimacy* 23
David gave a: E. F. Benson *David Blaize* 31
He crawled back: John Banville *Doctor Copernicus* 85
Words, words, words: William Shakespeare *Hamlet* (Yale) 60
Every morning: Thomas Bernhard *Prose* 125

150.

He looked forward: Colm Toibin *The Master* 233
Well, never mind: Plato *Gorgias* 13
We observe our: Thomas Dumm *Loneliness as a Way of Life* 98

⁍   10   ⁎

Back in the: Gore Vidal *Palimpsest* 385
Even the self-deprecating: Joseph P. Lash: *Eleanor and Franklin* 179
We spent the: Robert Bolaño *Amulet* 105
We discovered (very: Jorge Luis Borges *Collected Fictions* 68
Eleanor gave a: Ivy Compton-Burnett *Parents and Children* 69
She was wearing: John Fowles *The Magus* 14
It was that: James Joyce *Portrait of the Artist as a Young Man* 191
I viewed her: Andrew Holleran *Nights in Aruba* 40
She flung herself: Vladimir Nabokov *Laughter in the Dark* 62
"What a city: John Ashbery *Flow Chart* 189
Paris is the: Charles Henri Ford *Like Water from a Bucket* 208
When I look: David Lehman, ed. *Great American Prose Poems* 128
This is in: Conor Cruise O'Brien *Camus* 78
"Is it a: J. M. Coetzee *Waiting for the Barbarians* 84
 "Do you know: Gioia Timpanelli *Sometimes the Soul* 151
As if: Thomas Dumm *Loneliness as a Way of Life* 34
I rose from: Andrew Holleran *Nights in Aruba* 42
I've had it: Robert Bolaño *Amulet* 35
Let them think: John Francis Hunter *The Gay Insider* 26
But in France: Milan Kundera *Testaments Betrayed* 181
This is real: Adam Thirlwell *Delighted States* 88
Swarms of crows: Franz Kafka *The Castle* 11
The fact is: Huysmans *Against Nature* 181
To me it: William Shakespeare *Hamlet* (Yale) 63
"Well," she says: Justin Taylor *Everything Here is the Best Thing*

Ever 117

She moved in: Jean Genet *Querelle* 152

She was as: Georges Bataille *The Blue of Noon* 11

She was bizarre: John Fowles *The Magus* 14

"No means no: Bill Pronzini *The Hidden* 44

Perhaps you can: Theopile Gautier *Mademoiselle de Maupin* 97

"If you're hungry: Blair Niles *Strange Brother* 130

She went back: Rachel Ingalls *Mrs. Caliban* 63

Her thoughts were: Djuna Barnes *Nightwood* 76

She is inexhaustibly: Theopile *Gautier Mademoiselle de Maupin* 99

And though thee: Sylvia Townsend Warner *Summer Will Show* 87

Her eyes sparkled: Danilo Kiš *A Tomb for Boris* 8

What can I: Charles Burkhart *I. Compton-Burnett* 50

She did not: Carson McCullers *Member of the Wedding* 22

I understand: Plato *Collected Dialogues* 619

A woman whom: Colette *Pure and Impure* 43

I had been: Adam Phillips *Equals* 122

To poeticize oneself: Søren Kierkegaard *Diary of a Seducer* 112

It is something: Jacques Lacan *Four Fundamental Concepts of
     Psychoanalysis* 113

She turned: H. Rider Haggard *She* 231

"What have you: Henry Green *Doting* 42

She repeated all: Neil Bartlett *Ready to Catch Him* 198

For if there: Ronald Firbank *Three More Novels* 52

Imagine what that: Susan Sontag *I, etcetera: Stories* 144

"You think of: Jenny McPhee *A Man of No Moon* 208

She was really: Lydie Salvayre *Company of Ghosts* 15

I am nonviolent: John Francis Hunter *Gay Insider* 27

Luckily, the: Glen Baxter *Returns to Normal* (no page numbers)

It's still too: John Ashbery *April Galleons* 23

"I wish I: Noel Coward *Pomp and Circumstance* 49

The indifference in: Jorges Luis Borges *Collected Fictions* 284

What makes us: Adam Phillips *On Balance* 267
The evening ended: Glen Baxter *Returns to Normal* (no page numbers)
The great revolutions: Justin O'Brien *Camus* 34
If, as John: Adam Phillips *On Balance* 93

ᔥ 11 ᔥ

Now that the: Denton Welch *Maiden Voyage* 210
At night this: Alfred Chester *Looking for Genet* 172
Cars were rare: Justin Taylor *Everything Here is the Best Thing Ever* 3
The black cattle: Glenway Wescott *Continual Lessons* 175
Night music: Marlene Van Niekerk *Agaat* 2
Most of the: Clive Fisher *Hart Crane* 251
But the people: Elizabeth Gilbert *Last American Man* 215
The high cold: James Joyce *Dubliners* 33
2:00-5:00: Susan Sontag *Reborn* 17
The pen was: John Ashbery *April Galleons* 1
I could go: Joshua Mehigan *The Optimist* 58
I wrote about: Robert Bolaño *By Night in Chile* 84
Every book is: Helen Keller *The World I Live In* 14
How deep-seated: Glenway Wescott *Continual Lessons* 169
Like an earnest: Kenneth Burke *Towards a Better Life* 24
It is up: Charles Guignon *On Being Authentic* 130
These are the: Adam Phillips *On Balance* 236
They lived und: James Joyce *Finnegans Wake* 28
What a difference: Pascal *Pensees* 168
I am forever: John Francis Hunter *The Gay Insider* 78
Silly seasons: Harold Bloom *Anatomy of Influence* 13
Tinkering over sentences: David McConnell *Firebrat* 3
Lately, my sexual: Susan Sontag *I, etcetera: Stories* 45

Rick Whitaker

Revenge fucking: Michael Herr *Kubrick* 88

I felt excellent: Walter Kirn *My Hard Bargain* 103

Nonetheless my condition: David Markson *Wittgenstein's Mistress* 133

Loners can be: David McConnell *Firebrat* 3

It was all: Frederick Seidel *Poems 1959-2009* 9

Unending flights: W. G. Sebald *After Nature* 61

Other people see: Adam Phillips *On Balance* 224

I entered silently: Edmund White *Noctures for the King of Naples* 84

Then I stood: Daniel Kehlmann *Me and Kaminsky* 94

After that it: Graham Greene *May We Borrow Your Husband* 140

Writers are a: Justin O'Brien *Camus* 103

Our ears: Henry James *Portrait of a Lady* 311

The better you: D. H. Lawrence *Studies in Classic American Literature* 42

Yet I could: John Ashbery *Flow Chart* 178

I am beginning: Andre Gide *The Counterfeiters* 205

I have always: Elizabeth Hardwick *Sleepless Nights* 11

And this must: Ludwig Wittgenstein *Notebooks 1914-1916* 13

My mother's femaleness: Elizabeth Hardwick *Sleepless Nights* 21

My mother was: Georges Bataille *The Blue of Noon* 12

This was her: Dezso Kosztalanyi *Skylark* 15

And walking in: Djuna Barnes *Nightwood* 61

For nothing could: Lydie Salvayre *Company of Ghosts* 18

The dizziness and: E. F. Benson *The Freaks of Mayfair* 53

Women baffled me: Andrew Holleran *Nights in Aruba* 33

I was born: Wayne Koestenbaum *Moira Orfei in Aigues Mortes* 6

It was an: Mary McCarthy *The Group* 292

It was 1968: Paul Griffiths *Modern Music* 173

A sordid sexual: David McConnell *Firebrat* 81

From the beginning: Mikis Theodorakis *Journal of Resistance* 29

It's something almost: David Wojnarowicz *Memories That Smell*

Like Gasoline 47

Grown-ups tried: Jean-Christophe Valtat *03* 69

I was a: Jean Genet *The Declared Enemy* 8

My mother was: Andrew Holleran *Nights in Aruba* 33

Days and nights: Thomas Bernhard *Prose* 121

After I had: Denton Welch *Maiden Voyage* 7

I knew that: George Orwell *An Age Like This* 1

I became a: Richard Rodriguez *Brown* 147

Land of noble: Walicki *A History of Russian Thought* 75

New York City: Hart Crane *Library of America: Complete Poems and
    Selected Letters* 306

New York seemed: James Blake *The Joint* 309

Meanwhile, the possibility: Paul Griffiths *Modern Music* 150

Thank you, Proust: Michael Cunningham *By Nightfall* 17

I was glad: Denton Welch *Maiden Voyage* 35

Then the amazing: E. F. Benson *The Freaks of Mayfair* 111

My mother wanted: John Cheever *Stories* 691

"My dear," she: F. Scott Fitzgerald *The Great Gatsby* 40

My childhood was: Fran Lebowitz *Reader* 38

My mother has: Susan Sontag *I, etcetera: Stories* 133

My father went: Teju Cole *Open City* 188

Though long dead: Gore Vidal *Palimpsest* 256

Insanity, of course: Mark Rowlands *The Philosopher and the Wolf* 18

We find our: Charles Guignon *On Being Authentic* 87

"I didn't," said Joe: O. Henry *The Four Million* 67

My experience of: John Cage *Musicage* 60

Perhaps the least: Fran Lebowitz *Reader* 88

Yet any distinction: Harold Bloom *Anatomy of Influence* 4

Rick Whitaker

ຣວ 12 ຕຣ

David woke next: E. F. Benson *David Blaize* 34
He changed some: Vladimir Nabokov *Laughter in the Dark* 110
At all events: W. G. Sebald *Vertigo* 18
There were so: James Joyce *Dubliners* 107
He regarded himself: Kenneth Silverman *Begin Again* 88
He had many: Gioia Timpanelli *Sometimes the Soul* 154
It was a: James Joyce *Dubliners* 182
He tried to: James Joyce *Dubliners* 39
For the moment: Richard Ellmann *James Joyce* 66
He felt that: Vladimir Nabokov *Laughter in the Dark* 19
He had a: D. H. Lawrence *Sons and Lovers* 88
The idea of: Adam Phillips *On Balance* 224
I am sure: Ivy Compton-Burnett *A Family and a Fortune* 25
Which made it: Daniel Kehlmann *Measuring the World* 250
Mind you: Petros Abatzoglou *What Does Mrs. Freeman Want?* 94
His wife was: Dezso Kosztalanyi *Skylark* 79
But nobody came: Patrick White *Vivisector* 418
Obscurely, each thought: Bruce Duffy *The World As I Found It* 283
She noticed that: Henry James *Portrait of a Lady* 248
At such moments: W. G. Sebald *Vertigo* 28
It's corny: Michael Cunningham *By Nightfall* 16
"I suppose I: Blair Niles *Strange Brother* 221
The metaphor: Alex Ross *Listen to This* 16
I was still: Glen Baxter *The Further Blurtings of Glen Baxter* [no
     page numbers]
But one has: Jacques Lacan *Four Fundamental Concepts* 133
There are moments: R.P. Blackmur *Studies in Henry James* 197
It was all: Dezso Kosztalanyi *Skylark* 84
Moral: slack beds: Richard Howard *Inner Voices* 409
I rubbed his: Edmund White *My Lives* 239

156.

The poor man: Thomas Bernhard *My Prizes* 89
Still, he has: Mark Merlis *American Studies* 245
I didn't like: Michael Cunningham *By Nightfall* 22
I told him: Charles Henri Ford *Like Water From a Bucket* 149
A dreadful silence: E. F. Benson *Freaks of Mayfair* 123

ಬಿ 13 ೮೮

By late September: Ron Padgett *Joe* 216
He lived a: Frederick Seidel *Poems 1959-2009* 195
But he came: Gilbert Highet *Poets in a Landscape* 17
To travel without: Sylvia Townsend Warner *Summer Will Show* 85
One day while: Filip Noterdaeme *The Autobiography of Daniel J. Isengart* 45
He lay half: Patrick White *Vivisector* 448
We've been discussing: Susan Sontag *Reborn* 84
He slouched down: Gilbert Adair *Love and Death on Long Island* 132
"When I try: Ronald Firbank *Three More Novels* 36
The slight asymmetry: Edmund White *Rimbaud* 9
I liked being: Colette *Pure and Impure* 107
Those who meet: B. K. S. Iyengar *Light on Yoga* 45
"This," I said: Giacomo Casanova *History of My Life* 707
Believe it or: Bruce Duffy *The World As I Found It* 220
"Whoa, slow down: Edward St Aubyn *At Last* 114
"Do you really: Sylvia Townsend Warner *The Corner That Held Them* 56
All his life: Ron Padgett *Joe* 266
I exaggerate: Anita Brookner *Look at Me* 18
He never gave: Robert Walser *The Assistant* 281
That would be: Jane Gardam *Faith Fox* 81
But in general: Ron Padgett *Joe* 134

He waggled a: John Banville *The Untouchable* 139

"When one is: Ludwig Wittgenstein *Notebooks 1914-1916* 10

He was so: Robert Frost *The Notebooks of Robert Frost* 32

The sadness of: Sherwood Anderson *Winesburg, Ohio* 234

I could not: W. G. Sebald *Rings of Saturn* 5

He remembered his: Edna O'Brien *James Joyce* 12

In this he: Virginia Woolf *Orlando* 113

"Thank you for: D. H. Lawrence *Selected Letters* 307

Where did you: Bertolt Brecht *Galileo* 47

The book was: John Ashbery *April Galleons* 5

Joe had been: Ron Padgett *Joe* 52

It is all: D. H. Lawrence *Studies in Classic American Literature* 148

The price he: John Banville *The Untouchable* 268

It seemed to: Glen Baxter *Atlas* (no page numbers)

I am a: Alex Ross *Listen to This* 5

I felt myself: Anita Brookner *Look at Me* 87

That is how: J. M. Coetzee *Diary of a Bad Year* 91

Silence, he said: Virginia Woolf *Orlando* 93

We take long: James Merrill *The Changing Light at Sandover* 23

Sunshine, a bird: Roland Barthes *Mourning Diary* 166

Forced to make: Stephen Jay Gould *Hen's Teeth* 164

You never stop: Lydie Salvayre *The Power of Flies* 55

Apart from that: Jean Echenoz *Piano* 114

To all appearances: James Blake *The Joint* 157

Or maybe not: Jean Echenoz *Piano* 87

It was that: H. G. Wells *The Time Machine* 27

The other houses: James Joyce *Dubliners* 71

Joe said, "I'm: Peter Cameron *Someday This Pain* 34

Then he was: Sylvia Townsend Warner *Summer Will Show* 104

He wanted to: Bruce Duffy *The World As I Found It* 421

He believed that: Andrzej Walicki *A History of Russian Thought* 23

"All you've got: Hart Crane *Library of America: omplete Poems and*

Selected Letters 334

In other words: John Cage *Musicage* 61

You have to: Karl Ove Knausgaard *My Struggle: Book One* 188

I will not: David Levithan *The Full Spectrum* 108

Humility is a: E.M. Forster *Aspects of the Novel* 117

Our twentieth century: Robert Thurman *Inner Revolution* 37

The aim of: Harold Bloom *Ruin the Sacred Truths* 178

One last point: Gilbert Highet *Poets in a Landscape* 20

The future has: Diane Williams *It Was Like My Trying to Have a Tender-Hearted Nature* 91

Everyone today will: W. H. Auden *Forewords and Afterwords* 279

What a strange: David Leavitt *The Indian Clerk* 141

He dismissed bourgeois: Andrzej Walicki *History of Russian Thought* 80

Among the strongest: Edward Mendelson *Later Auden* 314

Everywhere, between the: Ronald Firbank *Three More Novels* 46

"The main thing: Ken Kesey *Sometimes a Great Notion* 177

I was stirred: Benjamin Sonnenberg *Lost Property* 135

Fortunately, I am: Anita Brookner *Look at Me* 36

"Well, yeah: Umberto Eco *Mysterious Flame* 348

"You know what: John Daido Loori *8 Gates of Zen* 59

If you care: David Thomson *Have You Seen...?* 25

"I don't," said: Charles Dickens *Barnaby Rudge* 10

"Who's your favorite: Alice Munro *The Progress of Love* 55

"Karl Ove Knausgaard: Karl Ove Knausgaard *My Struggle: Book Two* 496

Towards dark: Patrick White *The Vivisector* 448

I had been: Anita Brookner *Look at Me* 73

I of all: Umberto Eco *Mysterious Flame* 167

Loveless, landless: James Joyce *Ulysses* 43

Since this sensation: Geoff Dyer *Out of Sheer Rage: Wrestling with D. H. Lawrence* 51

Rick Whitaker

I Google it: Ellen Sussman *Dirty Words* 77
How quickly the: Louisa Perillo *I've Heard the Vultures Singing* 13
I found myself: H. G. Wells *The Time Machine* 56
All I could: W. G. Sebald *Rings of Saturn* 5
That's the ego: John Daido Loori *8 Gates of Zen* 59
Convinced life is: Frederick Seidel *Poems 1959-2009* 493

&ℭ 14 ℭℬ

An ambulance hurries: David Thomson *Have You Seen...?* 33
The crimes sparkle: Frederick Seidel *Area Code 212* 55
If only I: Susan Sontag *I, etcetera: Stories* 122
My intentions are: Max Ewing *Going Somewhere* 90
So much for: Sarah Bakewell *How to Live* 47
In this sense: James Wood *The Broken Estate* 256
"I'll teach you: Sam Massey *Return of the Greek* 119
That's a pledge: Max Ewing *Going Somewhere* 98
David laughed gleefully: Eleanor Porter *Just David* 94
He would love: James Joyce *Dubliners* 119
Such as...: Noel Coward *Pomp and Circumstance* 235
That indeed is: Harold Bloom *Hamlet: Poem Unlimited* 35
"There is happiness: Bertolt Brecht *Galileo* 42
Tilting his head: J. D. Salinger *Nine Stories* 47
"Please, do not: Alfred Chester *Jamie Is My Heart's Desire* 258
We all live: Ivy Compton-Burnett *A Family and a Fortune* 26
Do you know: Andre Tellier *Twilight Men* 31
"Nothing is got: Harold Bloom *Ruin the Sacred Truths* 201
The writer does: Roland Barthes *Critical Essays* xii
Thus every writer's: Roland Barthes *Reader* 405
I'd far rather: E. M. Forster *A Passage to India* 130
After all, it: Richard Rodriguez *Brown* 40

I was a: Charles Kaiser *The Gay Metropolis* 85

Punish me: James Joyce *Ulysses* 83

"You are quite: Thomas Hardy *Jude the Obscure* 152

"Things can always: Stephen Benatar *Wish Her Safe at Home* 7

"Ah": John Fowles *The Magus* 17

Longing for sweeter: John Daido Loori *8 Gates of Zen* 62

"I don't care: E. M. Forster *A Passage to India* 130

Very ingenious: George Orwell *An Age Like This* 20

And since, on: Lydie Salvayre *Portrait of the Artist as a Domesticated Animal* 70

A moment later: Evan S. Connell *Mrs. Bridge* 123

When I was: Robert Bolaño *By Night in Chile* 127

There was no: Glen Baxter *Returns to Normal* (no page numbers)

It was fascinating: Jean Echenoz *I'm Gone* 13

I work better: Gioia Timpanelli *Sometimes the Soul* 36

I forbade myself: Thomas Bernhard *My Prizes* 72

Leafing through a: Philip Roth *Professor of Desire* 201

ം 15 ൦ഭ

Eleanor "sprang from: Alison Weir *Eleanor of Acquitaine: A Life* 7

"If you want: Paula Fox *Poor George* 102

"I'm always kind: Henry James *Portrait of a Lady* 490

No one's supposed: Gore Vidal *Palimpsest* 129

I found it: Thomas Bernhard *My Prizes* 73

As a child: Gertrude Stein *Selections* ed., Retallack 17

Once she thought: AA Bronson *Lana* 151

At this point: E. F. Benson *The Freaks of Mayfair* 117

Flowering puberty: Aidan Higgins *Scenes from a Receding Past* 81

A great deal: David Lodge *Consciousness and the Novel* 91

There were stormy: Vladimir Nabokov *Laughter in the Dark* 192

And then, who: Jean Echenoz *Piano* 174
The struggle, if: Nathaniel Hawthorne *The Scarlet Letter* 177
Traits that we: Stephen Benatar *Wish Her Safe at Home* vi
She was under: Roland Barthes *S/Z* 229
Little is known: Polly Brooks *Queen Eleanor* 11
Eleanor took no: Ivy Compton-Burnett *Parents and Children* 164
"To wrestle with: William James *Talks to Teachers* 133
The paradox is: David Lodge *Consciousness and the Novel* 121
She stood in: Vladimir Nabokov *Laughter in the Dark* 42
Beside her was: Sylvia Townsend Warner *Summer Will Show* 95
He smiled wistfully: Ralph Sassone *The Intimates* 160
Eleanor loved the: Polly Brooks *Queen Eleanor* 12
Everything lay beneath: Robert Walser *The Assistant* 230
On such productive: Tony Judt *Memory Chalet* 9

ಬ 16 ಛ

I am sitting: Hans Keilson *Death of the Adversary* 37
Scared of the: Guy Hocquenghem *Screwball Asses* 38
Better take two: Michael Cunningham *By Nightfall* 5
The object in: Wayne Koestenbaum *Moira Orfei in Aigues Mortes* 14
Novels seem like: Amanda Michalapoulo *I'd Like* 41
The novel is: Don Paterson *Rain* 4
The worse your: Adam Phillips *On Balance* 33
Originality is therefore: Roland Barthes *Critical Essays* xii
Miracles happen every: H. Jackson Brown *Life's Little Instruction
    Book* 43
Each is in: Gilbert Highet *Poets in a Landscape* 14
Introspection, however, is: Ronald Firbank *Three More Novels* 55
Depression comes when: Roland Barthes *Mourning Diary* 62

ℬ 17 ℭ

David gave a: E. F. Benson *David Blaize* 46
"But where are: Jane Austen *Northanger Abbey* 161
At first, he: Gilbert Highet *Poets in a Landscape* 26
Suddenly their eyes: D. H. Lawrence *Sons and Lovers* 136
Now that this: Henry James *The Europeans* 48
Please, David, she: Rob Stephenson *Passes Through* 30
We only want: Philip Roth *Professor of Desire* 192
Now he's really: David Thomson *Have You Seen…?* 37
The deeper you: David Lodge *Consciousness and the Novel* 109
I was in: Victoria Redel *Loverboy* 21
I will not: James Joyce *Dubliners* 86
I remain a: Alfred Chester *Looking for Genet* 173
I returned to: J. M. Barrie *The White Bird* 98
"Oh, don't be: E. F. Benson *David Blaize* 45
For now was: Sylvia Townsend Warner *Summer Will Show* 90
As soon as: Gustave Flaubert *Sentimental Education* 69
The sense of: Graham Greene *The Heart of the Matter* 225
But instead of: Jean Genet *Querelle* 181
His life has: Søren Kierkegaard *Diary of a Seducer* 11
Poor, ridiculous young: Gilbert Highet *Poets in a Landscape* 25
"He has a: Aidan Higgins *Scenes from a Receding Past* 127
And David did: J. M. Barrie *The White Bird* 9
Everybody is feeling: Gertrude Stein *Wars I Have Seen* 75
They danced at: Aidan Higgins *Scenes from a Receding Past* 181
They attacked one: E. M. Forster *A Passage to India* 122
"Do you think: D. H. Lawrence *St. Mawr and the Man Who Died* 25
When it was: Nathanael West *Miss Lonelyhearts* 38
She hadn't said: Patricia Highsmith *Tremor of Forgery* 43
"What the hell: Paula Fox *The Coldest Winter* 51
"Do not talk: Ivy Comtpon-Burnett *Parents and Children* 19

163.

Rick Whitaker

What if, for: Edith Wharton *The Age of Innocence* 41
She spoke amiably: Edith Wharton *The Age of Innocence* 105
"Do you know: John Fowles *The Magus* 20
Somehow she managed: Paula Fox *The Coldest Winter* 42
It left her: Rachel Ingalls *Mrs. Caliban* 12
He listened carefully: Mark Merlis *American Studies* 115
"In future we'll: Gustave Flaubert *Sentimental Education* 124
The night was: Patrick White *The Vivisector* 445
They were young: Robert Bolaño *By Night in Chile* 83
One of the: W. Somerset Maugham *The Razor's Edge* 188
She spoke of: Charles Warren Stoddard *For the Pleasure of His Company* 181
Kindness personified: Glenway Wescott *Continual Lessons* 165
"The trouble is: Blair Niles *Strange Brother* 132
She really knows: Lydie Salvayre *The Company of Ghosts* 16
They agreed on: Charles Warren Stoddard *For the Pleasure of His Company* 88
"And now you: Ivy Compton-Burnett *Parents and Children* 276
One of the: Michael Cunningham *By Nightfall* 11
"Just like a: Hans Keilson *The Death of the Adversary* 17
She is nothing: Ray Monk *Ludwig Wittgenstein* 21
He withdraws again: Ralph Sassone *The Intimates* 35
Then there was: Virginia Woolf *Between the Acts* 3
"That's why I: Fyodor Dostoevsky *The Gambler* 158
"Amen," sang David: E. F. Benson *David Blaize* 28
Not knowing what: Nathanael West *Miss Lonelyhearts* 126
He hadn't meant: E. M. Forster *A Passage to India* 122
This scene was: Proust *Sodom and Gomorrah* (trans. Sturrock) 7
The Beautiful is: Charles Baudelaire *The Mirror of Art* 195
"You seem a: Anthony Burgess *A Clockwork Orange* 114
You look good: Alfred Chester *The Exquisite Corpse* 34
Don't insult me: Andre Gide *The Counterfeiters* 205

Throw me down: F. Scott Fitzgerald *The Great Gatsby* 144

Do you prefer: Theodore Dreiser *An American Tragedy* 465

He refused, but: Conor Cruise O'Brien *Camus* 103

"It's not out: Colette *Pure and Impure* 57

His contempt for: D. H. Lawrence *Stories* Vol. III 589

They thrill him: Michael Cunningham *By Nightfall* 5

She was so: Theodore Dreiser *An American Tragedy* 366

"But at the: Justin Spring *Secret Historian* 125

These are the: Adam Phillips *On Balance* 225

"I'm perfectly willing: Joseph P. Lash *Eleanor and Franklin* 684

"I wouldn't be: Darcy O'Brien *A Way of Life Like Any Other* 39

"It's true I'm: Philip Roth *Professor of Desire* 82

O dear, o: W. H. Auden *Forewords and Afterwords* 453

Colette had it: Bruce Duffy *The World As I Found It* 297

Thus women are: Ray Monk *Ludwig Wittgenstein* 22

Returning to the: Gustave Flaubert *Sentimental Education* 49

He kicked the: Alfred Chester *The Exquisite Corpse* 30

"What did I: Jean Echenoz *Piano* 167

"Well, what a: Ivy Compton-Burnett *Parents and Children* 149

She herself was: D. H. Lawrence *Sons and Lovers* 39

"Young people are: Gustave Flaubert *Sentimental Education* 74

"We are so: E. M. Forster *A Passage to India* 125

And his dark: Theodore Dreiser *An American Tragedy* 491

"Her voice is: F. Scott Fitzgerald *The Great Gatsby* 127

She took it: J. M. Coetzee *Diary of a Bad Year* 83

She came forward: Denton Welch *Maiden Voyage* 35

"And you really: Vladimir Nabokov *Laughter in the Dark* 100

The voice was: Dr. Seuss *Horton Hears a Who* (no page numbers)

This no longer: Frederick and Steven Barthelme *Double Down* 55

Once we have: Franz Kafka *Zurau* 28

Angry, and half: F. Scott Fitzgerald *The Great Gatsby* 186

We have to: Stephen Benatar *Wish Her Safe at Home* vi

Though I concealed: Kenneth Burke *Towards a Better Life* 21

We love women: Charles Baudelaire *Intimate Journals* 37

I went out: Aidan Higgins *Scenes from a Receding Past* 142

"You won't stay: Honoré de Balzac *Lost Illusions* 538

He spent the: Justin Spring *Secret Historian* 125

They need me: John Ashbery *April Galleons* 7

⁎ 18 ₧

"What are you: E. F. Benson *David Blaize* 215

He means to: Michael Cunningham *By Nightfall* 167

"Why, David," said: J. M. Barrie *The White Bird* 212

He'd spent half: Robert Walser *The Assistant* 285

The Magic Mountain: Michael Cunningham *By Nightfall* 7

He wished that: E. M. Forster *A Passage to India* 129

But it opens: Tony Judt *Memory Chalet* 90

The wish always: Adam Philips *Missing Out* 109

He had a: Carson McCullers *Reflections in a Golden Eye* 11

I gathered from: J. M. Barrie *The White Bird* 132

"Such missteps," he: Heinrich Kleist *Selected Prose* 269

I don't know: Tony Judt *Memory Chalet* 13

A kind of: Roland Barthes *Mourning Diary* 68

He wailed loudly: Sam Massey *Return of the Greek* 153

It was depressing: A. M. Homes *Jack* 134

"She loves me: Graham Greene *The Heart of the Matter* 235

Oh, incompetence!: Jorges Luis Borges *Collected Fictions* 32

If you can: Harold Bloom *Hamlet: Poem Unlimited* 32

I sigh, depressed: John Gardner *Grendel* 9

"Yes," I said: James Lasdun *The Horned Man* 101

I pulled myself: Diane Williams *It Was Like My Trying to Have a Tender-Hearted Nature* 14

166.

The more I: Van Gulden *Real Parents Real Children* 231

If a man's: B. K. S. Iyengar *Light on Yoga* 47

Love is an: Leo Bersani *A Future for Astyanax* 289

Such an old: John Banville *The Infinities* 8

Times like this: Louisa Perillo *I've Heard the Vultures Singing* 22

I'm just trying: Peter Cameron *Someday This Pain Will Be Useful To You* 32

This is not: Kazuki Sekida *Zen Training* 31

He dropped his: Theodore Dreiser *An American Tragedy* 528

"I'm sorry about: Andrew Holleran *Dancer from the Dance* 216

The supreme vice: *Portable Oscar Wilde* 511

David himself had: Andre Gide *The Counterfeiters* 165

He looked me: Gore Vidal *Two Sisters* 194

I knew I: Alfred Chester *The Exquisite Corpse* 52

"I pretended she: J. D. Salinger *Nine Stories* 13

But you see: Andrew Holleran *Dancer from the Dance* 169

What an unnatural: Leo Lerman *The Grand Surprise* 158

He was also: Clara Clement *Naples* 17

"The basis of: *Portable Oscar Wilde* 517

The mind obeys: Giacomo Casanova *History of My Life* 325

But maybe not: Adam Thirlwell *Delighted States* 11

All day long: Bruce Duffy *The World As I Found It* 247

I had not: Susanna Pinney, ed. *I'll Stand by You: Letters of Sylvia Townsend Warner* 24

My private life: Charles Kaiser *1968 in America* 200

We don't need: Gore Vidal *Two Sisters* 251

But think about: Stephen Jay Gould *Hen's Teeth* 170

One has to: Søren Kierkegaard *Diary of a Seducer* 45

No thanks: Harry Mathews *The Journalist* 55

David talked in: Don DeLillo *The Names* 261

"So I have: Søren Kierkegaard *Diary of a Seducer* 185

At least I: Gore Vidal *Palimpsest* 250

Rick Whitaker

That is our: Maximilien Robespierre *Virtue and Terror* 110
But a style: Adam Thirlwell *Delighted States* 24
"To tell the: Christopher Priest *The Glamour* 186
Oh, pardon, madame: Albert Camus *The Fall* 12
"Do you expect: J. M. Coetzee *Waiting for the Barbarians* 53
It was too: Rudy Wilson *The Red Truck* 143
The street is: Ralph Waldo Emerson *Essays* 257
The fairies perched: Sylvia Townsend Warner *Kingdoms of Elfin* 197
As long as: Guy Hocquenghem *Screwball Asses* 25
Young people: Tim Dean *Unlimited Intimacy* 162
I wanted to: Denton Welch *Maiden Voyage* 273
It was too: Anita Brookner *Look at Me* 46
In any modern: W. H. Auden *Forewords and Afterwords* 462
"All right, let's: Mary McCarthy *The Group* 313
The purpose is: Henry Green *Doting* 54
"I'd love to: Rachel Ingalls *Mrs. Caliban* 14
In the translucent: W. G. Sebald *After Nature* 63
"I can't tell: Ron Nyswaner *Blue Days Black Nights* 179
His warm, masculine: Robert Walser *The Assistant* 289
David's head dropped: Honoré de Balzac *Lost Illusions* 538
Added to this: Jean Echenoz *Piano* 135
"Why," I said: Andrew Holleran *Dancer from the Dance* 212
I threw him: Fyodor Dostoevsky *House of the Dead* 315
"I don't sleep: Sam Massey *Return of the Greek* 145
"What are you: Ralph Sassone *The Intimates* 159
It was an: Geoff Dyer *Out of Sheer Rage: Wrestling with D. H.
    Lawrence* 22
The intellectual attitude: Theodor Adorno *Stars Down to Earth* 157
I was astonished: Harry Mathews *The Journalist* 59
"What do you: Giacomo Casanova *History of My Life* 964
It's good at: John Gardner *Grendel* 10
"Doesn't matter what: E. F. Benson *David Blaize* 37

He was lying: Sylvia Townsend Warner *The Corner That Held Them* 36

He had given: Petros Abatzoglou *What Does Mrs. Freeman Want?* 102

He had never: Jorges Luis Borges *Collected Fictions* 366

It is not: Blackmur *Studies in Henry James* 199

"I wasn't trying: Victoria Redel *Border of Truth* 87

Nothing, however: D. H. Lawrence *Sons and Lovers* 137

For "style" has: Charles Baudelaire *Mirror of Art* 276

"Well, what is: Rudyard Kipling *Kim* 235

I heard some: James Lasdun *The Horned Man* 53

"Listen," he said: James Blake *The Joint* 167

Opportunity sometimes knocks: H. Jackson Brown *Life's Little Instruction Book* 123

Another long silence: Rudyard Kipling *Kim* 112

How the hell: Glenway Wescott *Continual Lessons* 161

We should strive: Andre Tellier *Twilight Men* 112

But I am: H. G. Wells *The Time Machine* 104

ଔ 19 ଓ

Strange beds have: Kazuo Ishiguro *Remains of the Day* 47

A spot of: Proust *Sodom and Gomorrah* 55

I was—and: Lydie Salvayre *Portrait of the Artist as a Domesticated Animal* 26

Was love insane: Andre Tellier *Twilight Men* 91

I, too, wanted: Edmund White *Rimbaud* 7

I know the: Alex Ross *Listen to This* 19

I, too, wanted: Edmund White *Rimbaud* 7

David sat quietly: Don DeLillo *The Names* 67

"Anarchy," he said: Graham Greene *May We Borrow Your Husband?* 126

Rick Whitaker

I made no: Jean Genet *Funeral Rites* 14
My mind drifts: Alex Ross *Listen to This* 20
Life in the: Andre Tellier *Twilight Men* 88
It was too: Patrick White *Vivisector* 458
Yet the vulnerable: Gilbert Adair *Love and Death on Long Island* 134
"I have no: Vladimir Nabokov *Laughter in the Dark* 44
I say that: David Lehman, ed. *Great American Prose Poems* 146
Life has but: Charles Baudelaire *Intimate Journals* 39
"I like men: *Portable Oscar Wilde* 342
"There's a something: Henry James *The Lesson of The Master* 49
He said that: Giacomo Casanova *History of My Life* 568
Tentatively, he added: David McConnell *Firebrat* 94
Then he smiled: Vladimir Nabokov *Laughter in the Dark* 34
He liked to: Robert Lowell *Collected Prose* xi
In truth, however: Sarah Bakewell *How to Live* 53
Behind our thoughts: Ludwig Wittgenstein *Notebooks 1914-1916* 22
He raised his: Mark Merlis *American Studies* 114
I ignored this: Stephen Benatar *Wish Her Safe at Home* 16
 "I must kiss: Henry Green *Doting* 194
"One night," he: Alfred Chester *The Exquisite Corpse* 33
He was a: Rudyard Kipling *Kim* 93
Sexy: John Francis Hunter *The Gay Insider* 425
His favorite instrument: Thomas Bernhard *Gargoyles* 76
A local artist: Edmund White *Rimbaud* 130
Asleep, or perhaps: Andre Tellier *Twilight Men* 71
He picked up: Robert Walser *The Assistant* 295
The men I: Carl Van Vechten *Parties* 157
That can hardly: Bertolt Brecht *Galileo* 30
I wish I: Glenn Gould *Letters* 240
As Gertrude Stein: Janet Malcolm *Two Lives* 224

ဆ 20 previously cg

You can imagine: Thomas Bernhard *Frost* 33
This is Eleanor's: Alison Weir *Eleanor of Acquitaine* 2
Her whole life: Janet Malcolm *Two Lives*14
Life-bloated: John Gardner *Grendel* 11
She was woebegone: Jean Genet *Funeral Rites* 12
She has given: Gore Vidal *Two Sisters* 172
When she walked: Hans Keilson *Comedy in a Minor Key* 81
"The force of: Sylvia Townsend Warner *Summer Will Show* 79
"Ridiculous," she said: Hans Keilson *Comedy in a Minor Key* 82
Meanwhile, she also: Sylivia Townsend Warner *The Corner That Held Them* 76
We can't talk: Justin Taylor *Everything Here is the Best Thing Ever* 124
Tears brimmed up: Menis Koumandereas *Koula* 86
To be continued: James Joyce *Finnegans Wake* 18
She talks about: Just Taylor *Everything Here is the Best Thing Ever* 114
Some situations brought: Joseph P. Lash *Eleanor and Franklin* 145
No one can: W. G. Sebald *Austerlitz* 25
She had no: D. H. Lawrence *St. Mawr* 55
She was thirty-one: D. H. Lawrence *Sons and Lovers* 2
They had married: D. H. Lawrence *Stories* Vol I 71
It was the: Evan S. Connell *Mrs. Bridge* 125
His rosy tongue: Ronald Firbank *Five Novels* 372
He and his: Gilbert Highet *Poets in a Landscape* 25
His hatred of: Gustave Flaubert *Sentimental Education* 202
Exalted but remote: Edmund White *Rimbaud* 141
Whenever he went: Vladimir Nabokov *Laughter in the Dark* 36
He was desperate: Edmund White *Rimbaud* 146
She had cried: Henry James *Portrait of a Lady* 358
After that she: Gilbert Highet *Poets in a Landscape* 25
There was nothing: Karl Ove Knausgaard *My Struggle: Book Two* 206

She walked on: Sylvia Townsend Warner *Summer Will Show* 102
I remarked in: Edmund White *Nocturnes for the King of Naples* 130
We had sex: Matthew Stadler *Allan Stein* 27
I've never cultivated: Henry James *Portrait of a Lady* 484
Later she was: Gilbert Highet *Poets in a Landscape* 166
If there was: Sarah Bakewell *How to Live* 48
"I had an: Mary McCarthy *The Group* 312
She expected that: Christopher Bollas *The Shadow of the Object* 125
"Then I went: Charles Kaiser *1968 in America* 188
She looked at: Robert Bolaño *By Night in Chile* 113
Mentally, I rolled: Karl Ove Knausgaard *My Struggle: Book Two* 372
I didn't love: Graham Greene *Travels with My Aunt* 21
Alone unchanging: Ronald Firbank *Five Novels* 372

ᏸ 21 ෬

Something very strange: Noel Coward *Lyrics* 381
You know what: Justin Taylor *Everything Here is the Best Thing
    Ever* 116
Desirelessness: J. D. Salinger *Franny and Zooey* 198
So one day: Jonathan Ames *I Love You* 120
"Do come in: Barbara Pym *Jane and Prudence* 146
I make sure: Jean Genet *The Declared Enemy: Texts and Interviews* 12
It was like: Sylvia Townsend Warner *Summer Will Show* 108
The result is: Shunryu Suzuki *Zen Mind, Beginner's Mind* 39
Are you constantly: Daniel C. Dennett *Consciousness Explained* 137
How much time: E. M. Forster *Aspects of the Novel* 50
It is some: Janet Malcolm *Two Lives* 132
This is Freud's: Adam Phillips *On Balance* 179
Noon slumbers: James Joyce *Ulysses* 42

ℬ 22 ℭ

A high-class: Geoff Dyer *Out of Sheer Rage: Wrestling with D. H. Lawrence* 55

There, milling about: Roland Barthes *S/Z* 221

People had to: Hart Crane *Library of America Collected Poems and Selected Letters* 293

The mostly faded: Hans Keilson *Comedy in a Minor Key* 83

It was the: Robert Bolaño *Amulet* 50

Champagne does wonders: Lydie Salvayre *The Award* 66

"But, what am: Djuna Barnes *Nightwood* 78

Here we have: Lydie Salvayre *The Award* 71

Like all the: Sherwood Anderson *Winesburg, Ohio* 135

Whereas what I: Gordon Lish *Zimzum* 54

We all love: Daniel C. Dennett *Consciousness Explained* 23

We sat for: Peter Cameron *Someday This Pain Will Be Useful To You* 32

"Listen, my dear: Noel Coward *Pomp and Circumstance* 114

"You mustn't be: J. M. Coetzee *Waiting for the Barbarians* 51

Eleanor was silent: Ivy Compton-Burnett *Parents and Children* 31

"To forgive, it: Charles Burkhart *I. Compton-Burnett* 13

"Yes, I can: Colm Toibin *The Master* 206

I was having: Gary Krist *The Garden State* 139

"The ancients have: Amy Hempel *Reasons To Live* 47

I wanted to: David Lehman, ed. *Great American Prose Poems* 293

"What every man: Glenway Wescott *Continual Lessons* 359

And I confess: Lydie Salvayre *Power of Flies* 65

Essentially, we would: Leo Bersani *A Future for Astyanax* 302

The whole point: Susan Sontag *Reborn* 81

It is only: Noel Coward *Pomp and Circumstance* 124

I disapprove of: Evan S. Connell *Mrs. Bridge* 8

If you're going: Fran Lebowitz *Reader* 120

Eleanor laughed: Ann Weil *Eleanor Roosevelt: Fighter for Social Justice* 13

She stopped abruptly: Sylvia Townsend Warner *Summer Will Show* 102

She gave a: James Lasdun *The Horned Man* 52

"I love this: David McConnell *Firebrat* 122

She is elegantly: W. G. Sebald *Unrecounted* 94

Right now, finally: Justin Taylor *Everything Here is the Best Thing Ever* 13

All at once: David Levithan *The Full Spectrum* 165

Then something opened: John Banville *The Untouchable* 276

"My dear Eleanor: Jane Austen *Northanger Abbey* 102

Finally, much exasperated: Alfred Chester *Jamie Is My Heart's Desire* 252

"If you ever: J. D. Salinger *Nine Stories* 31

I don't know: Richard Rodriguez *Brown* 92

She could sit: D. H. Lawrence *Stories* Vol III 647

Ketchup on nearly: Sherrie Eldridge *20 Things Adopted Kids Wish Their Adoptive Parents Knew* 20

Neither of us: Justin Taylor *Everything Here is the Best Thing Ever* 12

"Wouldn't you like: J. M. Coetzee *Waiting for the Barbarians* 89

She was one: V. S. Pritchett *Dead Man Leading* 25

"But I hate: Kenneth Silverman *Begin Again* 87

She is a: Stephen Benatar *Wish Her Safe at Home* vi

"I could use: Justin Taylor *Everything Here is the Best Thing Ever* 12

"When I was: Sherrie Eldridge *20 Things Adopted Kids Wish Their Adoptive Parents Knew* 26

It was a: Mark Epstein *Psychotherapy without the Self: A Buddhist Perspective* 194

ଅ 23 ଓଃ

I drank two: Wayne Koestenbaum *Moira Orfei in Aigues Mortes* 23

I've pulled a lot: Jonathan Ames *I Love You* 119

Now I am: Walter Benjamin *Illuminations* 67

I flinched when: Brane Mozetic *Banalities* 17

Writing is a: Cyril Connolly *The Condemned Playground* 63

This night was: David Levithan *The Full Spectrum* 187

I sat still: Rob Stephenson *Passes Through* 24

The dahlias were: Jean Genet *Funeral Rites* 32

My father is: Sylvia Townsend Warner *Summer Will Show* 81

He arrived late: Brane Mozetic *Banalities* 5

One of his: Danilo Kiš *Encyclopedia of the Dead* 3

Understand that I: Teju Cole *Open City* 188

A father who: Marie Chaix *The Laurels of Lake Constance* 17

Occultism is the: Theodor Adorno *Stars Down to Earth* 175

I have been: John Banville *The Untouchable* 307

Think of the: Frederick Seidel *Area Code 212* 7

That's corruption: Robert Frost *The Notebooks of Robert Frost* 51

From fifteen on: Gertrude Stein *Wars I Have Seen* 30

But how can: Leo Bersani *A Future for Astyanax* 167

"Why am I: Hugh Kenner *The Pound Era* 24

With history piling: David Lehman, ed. *Great American Prose Poems* 151

These questions carry: W. G. Sebald *After Nature* 106

Should a homosexual: Leo Bersani *Homos* 113

That's the thing: Edmund Wilson *Axel's Castle* 236

If I had: Albert Camus *The Fall* 21

"The hero is: Bertolt Brecht *Galileo* 66

The sooner the: J. M. Coetzee *Waiting for the Barbarians* 77

Jesus wept: James Joyce *Ulysses* 38

No spirit exists: Theodor Adorno *Stars Down to Earth* 179

Rick Whitaker

I surprised myself: Alfred Chester *Jamie is My Heart's Desire* 31
I don't have: Rebecca Godfrey *The Torn Skirt* 181
I could use: Wayne Koestenbaum *Moira Orfei in Aigues Mortes* 32
Summertime shudders: Richard Strauss *Four Last Songs* II.
    (Hesse)
Four days pass: David Leavitt *The Indian Clerk* 281
"I need some: Colm Tobin *The Master* 302
This is not: Theodor Adorno *Stars Down to Earth* 181
"If you get: Alfred Chester *The Exquisite Corpse* 178
Thanks for everything: Justin Spring *Secret Historian* 158
The solitude was: Harry Mathews *The Journalist* 5
I want to: Mark Scott *A Bedroom Occupation* 62
But nobody comes: Franz Kafka *The Complete Stories* 337

ဆ 24 ဆ

Because Joe was: Ron Padgett *Joe* 185
Joe answered: Ron Padgett *Joe* 63
As compensation what: Charles Dickens *Great Expectations* 164
Ignorant and lazy: James Merrill *The Changing Light at Sandover* 15
"Come and sit: D. H. Lawrence *Collected Stories* Vol IV 1104
He is the: *Addicted: Notes from the Belly of the Beast* (Whitaker) 200
"In a recent: Adam Phillips *On Balance* 162
Yes, he says: Sarah Bakewell *How to Live* 53
The reasonable man: Edna O'Brien *James Joyce* 224
"You cannot train: Edward Mendelson *Early Auden* 20
That, I think: Adam Thirwell *Delighted States* 26
As the nineteenth-century: Sarah Bakewell *How to Live* 53
He was soon: Joseph P. Lash *Eleanor and Franklin* 386
For too many: Marion Meade *Eleanor of Acquitaine* 267
"I do hope: Douglas Crase *Both* 195

A letter from: Joseph P. Lash *Eleanor and Franklin* 345
She felt that: Jack London *The Game* 92
"Come to Spain: Barbara Pym *Jane and Prudence* 200
"You know, Joe: D. H. Lawrence *Collected Stories* Vol IV 1111
Women are not: Henry James *Portrait of a Lady* 247
There is, I: Fran Lebowitz *Reader* 105
"What about this: Patrick White *Vivisector* 419
The next day: D. H. Lawrence *Sons and Lovers* 105
Her gaiety had: Robert Walser *The Assistant* 156
She behaved flawlessly: Edna O'Brien *James Joyce* 148
"Hello, sweetheart: J. D. Salinger *Franny and Zooey* 188
You see I: Edith Wharton *The Age of Innocence* 21
"As you know: Colm Tobin *The Master* 265
I doubted that: Binnie Kirshenbaum *Pure Poetry* 49
"All my life: Charles Kaiser *The Gay Metropolis* 192
Certainly there was: Proust *Sodom and Gomorrah* 52
Maybe a chemical: David Gilbert *Remote Feed* 206
For Eleanor, the: Marion Meade *Eleanor of Acquitaine* 238
Presently the lad: D. H. Lawrence *Sons and Lovers* 4
She said a: Paula Fox *The Coldest Winter* 78
That is when: Ralph Sassone *The Intimates* 35
He was still: Richard Ellmann *James Joyce* 139
She is absurdly: John Banville *The Infinities* 69
A dim antagonism: James Joyce *Portrait of the Artist as a Young
    Man* 218
Her eyes, however: Henry James *Portrait of a Lady* 150
But Joe said: James Joyce *Dubliners* 173
He has a: Richard Ellmann *James Joyce* 137
"I need a: John Banville *The Untouchable* 274
The more clearly: Patrick White *Vivisector* 424
"Yes," she sighed: Patrick White *Vivisector* 436
"So there'll be: Rachel Ingalls *Mrs. Caliban* 80

Strange words to: J. M. Coetzee *Elizabeth Costello* 28

"Look here," he: Sherwood Anderson *Winesburg, Ohio* 141

"A person's a: Dr. Seuss *Horton Hears a Who* (no page numbers)

So adult did: Evan S. Connell *Mrs. Bridge* 11

Then, on a: J. D. Salinger *Franny and Zooey* 134

The ways of women: David Leavitt *The Indian Clerk* 282

This was a: Charles Dickens *Great Expectations* 80

"I just can't: T. J. Parsell *Fish* 290

"She thinks I'm: Sherwood Anderson *Winesburg, Ohio* 206

We have heard: Alex Ross *The Rest is Noise* 541

Later Joe was: Ron Padgett *Joe* 14

He was one: Vladimir Nabokov *Laughter in the Dark* 72

He's a funny: David Gilbert *Remote Feed* 88

Normality is a: Herbert Marcuse *Eros and Civilization* 246

But many things: Franz Kafka *The Complete Stories* 286

Inadequate as he: Sarah Bakewell *How to Live* 54

His waking hours: Edmund White *Nocturnes for the King of
    Naples* 130

Time would take: Evan S. Connell *Mrs. Bridge* 23

But few people: Richard Ellmann *James Joyce* 138

"Oh, I know: John Banville *The Untouchable* 209

Joe shuffled down: Sarah Schulman *The Child* 18

"Let me deceive: Giacomo Casanova *History of My Life* 1137

Going upstairs, the: Patrick White *Vivisector* 456

"Dad understands that: Kenneth Silverman *Begin Again* 86

This rings absolutely: Gore Vidal *Inventing a Nation* 175

"What should I: Paula Fox *The Coldest Winter* 68

"That's just what: Charles Dickens *Great Expectations* 168

Even as they: John Ashbery *April Galleons* 2

Her influence over: Edna O'Brien *James Joyce* 135

Is dead: Christopher Isherwood *A Single Man* 13

He was destined: James Joyce *Portrait of the Artist as a Young Man* 219

Eleanor did not: Bertolt Brecht *Galileo* 81
"He was born: Amanda Michalopoulo *I'd Like* 112
How can they: Michael Cunningham *By Nightfall* 31
She builds an: Stephen Benatar *Wish Her Safe at Home* ix
Eleanor's view prevailed: Joseph P. Lash *Eleanor and Franklin* 175
It was life: James Joyce *Finnegans Wake* 478
Silence: Mikis Theodorakis *Journal of Resistance* 155
Now that's what: Sam Massey *Return of the Greek* 45

⁎ 25 ℞

"Well, this would: F. Scott Fitzgerald *The Great Gatsby* 88
There is a woman: Susan Sontag *I, etcetera: Stories* 15
David closed his: Eleanor Porter *Just David* 193
"Life has been: Colm Tobin *The Master* 230
"Sounds dreadful: Evan S. Connell *Mrs. Bridge* 27
He was smoking: Mary McCarthy *The Group* 159
He was freshly: Colm Tobin *The Master* 220
And it begins: David Thomson *Have You Seen…?* 37
Style is an: H. G. Wells *The Time Machine* 78
I turned on: James Lasdun *Horned Man* 41
Nothing and everything: Edna O'Brien *James Joyce* 16
"Chopin, eh?: David Leavitt *The Indian Clerk* 127
It was Stravinsky: Alan Bennett *Writing Home* 39
Despite everything that: Ben Marcus *Notable American Women* 70
Messages from an: Alan Bennett *Writing Home* 229
And then there's: Elizabeth Gilbert *Last American Man* 217
To cook is: Shunryu Suzuki *Zen Mind, Beginner's Mind* 53
How much my: Franz Kafka *The Complete Stories* 285
Every moment it: Montaigne *Selected Essays* 25
At this moment: Honoré de Balzac *Lost Illusions* 611

"Darling, is there: Andrew Holleran *Dancer from the Dance* 217

To this crucial: Lydie Salvayre *The Award* 74

"Oh God," he: Andrew Holleran *Dancer from the Dance* 104

Every time he: Sherwood Anderson *Winesburg, Ohio* 144

He is ill-mannered: Edmund Wilson *Axel's Castle* 79

Seen from a: Alex Ross *The Rest is Noise* 527

He tops, for: Justin Taylor *Everything Here is the Best Thing Ever* 119

I consider my: Rebecca Godfrey *The Torn Skirt* 164

It is made: Hugh Kenner *The Pound Era* 182

Just a few: *Addicted: Notes from the Belly of the Beast* (Whitaker) 193

And that's what: Adam Phillips *On Balance* 223

That's just the: Denis Donoghue *American Classics* 234

How was it: Edmund Wilson *Axel's Castle* 139

You're always hearing: Binne Kirshenbaum *Pure Poetry* 49

Such are the: James Lasdun *Horned Man* 61

There are moments: Thomas Dumm *Loneliness as a Way of Life* 12

In the real: John Ashbery *Flow Chart* 197

I remember that: Rudyard Kipling *Kim* 259

But, in all: James Blake *The Joint* 155

To be is: Hugh Kenner *The Pound Era* 164

David, at the: Eleanor Porter *Just David* 88

"Do you want: J. D. Salinger *Franny and Zooey* 147

I came here: Sherwood Anderson *Winesburg, Ohio* 162

Funny is almost: Justin Taylor *Everything Here is the Best Thing Ever* 136

David was one: Honoré de Balzac *Lost Illusions* 567

"Is it naïve: Elizabeth Gilbert *Last American Man* 254

He kissed my: T. J. Parsell *Fish* 160

"I cannot tell: George Eliot *Middlemarch* 18

Indeed, I thought: Heinrich Kleist *Selected Prose* 267

He began to: W. Somerset Maugham *The Razor's Edge* 141

But in a: Richard Wollheim *Painting as an Art* 285

"I was once: Mary Jo Bang/Dante *The Inferno* 17

This had never: Charles Kaiser *The Gay Metropolis* 198

Is he just: Michael Cunningham *By Nightfall* 6

"I was not: Giacomo Casanova *History of My Life* 685

David was radically: E. F. Benson *David Blaize* 301

"David, you are: Philip Roth *Professor of Desire* 125

"I'm beginning to: Brenda McCreight *Parenting Your Adopted
    Older Child* 189

Is that not: James Joyce *Portrait of the Artist as a Young Man* 137

David smiles, shyly: John Waters *Role Models* 225

How well I'm: Justin Spring *Secret Historian* 169

David had been: John Waters *Role Models* 221

"Fertilize your inner: Lydie Salvayre *The Award* 76

"Shall we speak: Bertolt Brecht *Galileo* 89

Who wrote this: David Gilbert *Remote Feed* 152

Dinner was not: Bruce Duffy *The World As I Found It* 450

Far from it: Søren Kierkegaard Works of Love 219

To put it: D. A. Powell and David Trinidad *By Myself* 1

He suffered tortures: D. H. Lawrence *Sons and Lovers* 330

From there on: Geoff Dyer *Out of Sheer Rage: Wrestling with D. H.
    Lawrence* 26

I left him: J. D. Salinger *Franny and Zooey* 141

The end of: Henry James *Portrait of a Lady* 130

Something must be: Brane Mozetic *Banalities* 18

He selected a: Andre Tellier *Twilight Men* 57

"I know how: Stephen Benatar *Wish Her Safe at Home* 13

And so the: Anthony Burgess *A Clockwork Orange* 33

I will not: James Joyce *Portrait of the Artist as a Young Man* 113

But the Milky: H. G. Wells *The Time Machine* 106

That is the: Fritz Zorn *Mars* 241

That is how: Hugh Kenner *The Pound Era* 5

It is too: Frederick Seidel *Poems 1959-2009* 411

Writing is no: Roland Barthes *Mourning Diary* 230
Too late: Milan Kundera *Testaments Betrayed* 191
Of all the: Fritz Zorn *Mars* 154
The light that: Andre Tellier *Twilight Men* 50
No man knows: Montaigne *Selected Essays* 22

℠ 26 ℞

All my life: Fritz Zorn *Mars* 134
It called for: Fritz Zorn *Mars* 41
The psychologists know: Lynne Sharon Schwartz *Emergence of Memory* 46
But I'm very: Virginia Woolf *Diaries* Vol V 306
I don't want: David Levithan *The Full Spectrum* 186
One thing is: Gregory Woods *History of Gay Literature* 340
Given how our: Gregory Woods *History of Gay Literature* 386
A friend of: Richard Rodriguez *Brown* 217
The fairies broke: Sylvia Townsend Warner *Kingdoms of Elfin* 199
Life mirrors art: Binnie Kirshenbaum *Pure Poetry* 52
This tickles Joe: Ken Kesey *Sometimes a Great Notion* 176
"He must have: Rachel Ingalls *Mrs Caliban* 20
What other point: Michael Warner *The Trouble with Normal* 196
Life in New York: John Ashbery *April Galleons* 32
"And I want: Kenzburo Oe *A Quiet Life* 86
My conscience pricked: Susanna Pinney, ed. *I'll Stand by You: Letters of Sylvia Townsend Warner* 7
I wanted to: George Orwell *An Age Like This* 3
And I can: Guy Hocquenghm *Screwball Asses* 60

ℬ 27 ℬ

I must have: Franz Kafka *The Complete Stories* 278

David was sitting: J. M. Barrie *The White Bird* 43

Had they remained: Geoff Dyer *Out of Sheer Rage: Wrestling with D. H. Lawrence* 52

As he had: Gustave Flaubert *Sentimental Education* 212

"I suffer every: Giacomo Casanova *History of My Life* 664

It takes ages: Brane Mozetic *Banalities* 21

To which David: J. M. Barrie *The White Bird* 102

I think that: Plato *Collected Dialogues* 76

He is tortured: Montaigne *Selected Essays* 20

My real type: John Waters *Role Models* 229

Meaning is never: Roland Barthes *Reader* xvii

But in the: Michael Warner *The Trouble with Normal* 17

It hurts: Brane Mozetic *Banalities* 28

I don't know: Jonathan Ames *I Love You* 161

David sighs: John Waters *Role Models* 224

"Turn over here: Sam Massey *Return of the Greek* 116

He puts on: Ludwig Wittgenstein *Lectures 1932-35* 63

"Maybe you're ready: David McConnell *Firebrat* 127

He lay on: Alfred Chester *The Exquisite Corpse* 30

He's a man: Jean Genet *The Declared Enemy* 12

"Go to hell: Ernest Hemingway *A Farewell to Arms* 32

This is the: Thomas Bernhard *My Prizes* 77

To me the: Gore Vidal *Two Sisters* 126

We never release: Denis Donoghue *American Classics* 191

At any rate: Thomas Bernhard *My Prizes* 98

I had to: David McConnell *Firebrat* 235

ଝ 28 ଔ

The cocks are: Mikis Theodorakis *Journal of Resistance* 156

It is like: John Koethe *Poetry at One Remove* 12

Christmas was approaching: Robert Walser *The Assistant* 271

Joe slept on: Ron Padgett *Joe* 60

He hears nothing: Michel de Ghelderode *7 Plays* 242

This was a: Evan S. Connell *Mrs. Bridge* 124

Like many people: Doug Crase *Both* 237

"You don't know: Honoré de Balzac *Lost Illusions* 536

He had his: James Joyce *Portrait of the Artist as a Young Man* 144

"I wish we: Ivy Compton-Burnett *A Family and a Fortune* 27

This, he insisted: Kenneth Burke *Towards a Better Life* 7

"Poor boy!: Honoré de Balzac *Lost Illusions* 500

"You won't believe: Justin Taylor *Everything Here is the Best Thing Ever* 11

At the risk: Stepehn Jay Gould *Hen's Teeth* 133

David drank slowly: Don DeLillo *The Names* 219

He was a: Gilbert Highet *Poets in a Landcsape* 137

It had brought: Marion Meade *Eleanor of Acquitaine* 189

The Romantic is: Edmund Wilson *Axel's Castle* 10

Etc, etc: Gordon Lish *Collected Fictions* 21

I suppose it: Christopher Bollas *The Shadow of the Object* 257

The sex with: James Blake *The Joint* 355

Desire was his: Bruce Duffy *The World As I Found It* 31

Seeing Dick Cheney: David Wojnarowicz *Memories That Smell Like Gasoline* 44

Joe and I: Charles Dickens *Great Expectations* 160

Television is a: George W. S. Trow *In the Context of No Context* 45

The vivid rhetoric: Susan Howe *My Emily Dickinson* 46

"Don't lose your: Charles Dickens *Great Expectations* 131

"He should have: Rachel Ingalls *Mrs. Caliban* 16

You took the: James Joyce *Finnegans Wake* 66

I'm getting so: Hart Crane *Library of America: Collected Poems and Selected Letters* 370

Joyce is right: James Baldwin *Notes of a Native Son* 162

History makes me: Rob Stephenson *Passes Through* 37

I thought: Gordon Lish *Collected Fictions* 60

I am all: David Wojnarowicz *Memories That Smell Like Gasoline* 60

There is no: Fran Lebowitz *Reader* 12

Must be the: David Wojnarowicz *Memories That Smell Like Gasoline* 43

It's right before: Lydie Salvayre *Power of Flies* 157

"Dad," he says: David Gilbert *Remote Feed* 95

"Don't worry": Ron Padgett *Joe* 85

"OK, OK": Rachel Ingalls *Mrs. Caliban* 24

I do not: Willa Cather *Death Comes for the Archbishop* 50

My dear child: Bertolt Brecht *Galileo* 69

ॐ 29 ☙

David introduced me: Don DeLillo *The Names* 6

He was not: Charles Henri Ford *Like Water from a Bucket* 156

It was a: D. H. Lawrence *Sons and Lovers* 5

In all things: Donald keene *The Pleasures of Japanese Literature* 7

Or was I: Nicholson Baker *Room Temperature* 11

I stared at: Paula Fox *The Coldest Winter* 57

He was tall: Albert Camus *The Plague* 146

He had a: Jane Gardam *Faith Fox* 133

In his left: Danilo Kiš *Encyclopedia of the Dead* 3

He's a former: James Blake *The Joint* 90

For all I: Henry James *Portrait of a Lady* 497

Perhaps the man: D. H. Lawrence *Stories* Vol I 96

He also struck: Anita Brookner *Look at Me* 73

The handshake of: Helen Keller *The World I Live In* 9

There are some: Charles Warren Stoddard *For the Pleasure of His
Company* 29

A single insight: Samuel Beckett *Nohow On* 85

As a child: Robert Frost *The Notebooks of Robert Frost* 30

And so on: Danilo Kiš *Encyclopedia of the Dead* 7

He was one: Edgar Saltus *Mr Incoul's Misadventure* 3

His bald head: Michael Cunningham *By Nightfall* 7

He stared at: Emilio Lascano Tegui *On Elegance While Sleeping* 13

The signs of: Dezso Kosztalanyi *Skylark* 77

There was a: Jane Gardam *Faith Fox* 100

"I suppose I'm: Patricia Highsmith *Tremor of Forgery* 244

I was just: T. J. Parsell *Fish* 154

A bitch: Ronald Firbank *Five Novels* 373

David said he: E. F. Benson *David Blaize* 311

Dandruff dusted the: Kosztal Sklyark 76

"David, what is: Philip Roth *Professor of Desire* 114

The young man: Richard Rodriguez *Brown* 223

"David told me: Philip Roth *Professor of Desire* 233

His voice was: Sylvia Townsend Warner *Summer Will Show* 114

He uses a language: Thomas Bernhard *Gargoyles* 97

"Ah, they're part: Henry James *Portrait of a Lady* 247

Sometimes not so: Edward Mendelson *Later Auden* 306

"It's regrettable, but: Julia Kristeva *Colette* 18

Oh, honey, don't: Truman Capote *Music for Chameleons* 195

So alone, in: Mark Merlis *American Studies* 181

"We met on: Don DeLillo *The Names* 265

Ridiculous: Hart Crane *Library of America: Collected Poems and
Selected Letters* 295

He went from: Andrew Holleran *Dancer from the Dance* 128

Our flesh shrinks: James Joyce *Portrait of the Artist as a Young Man* 142

But the fear: Gustave Flaubert *Sentimental Education* 216
Being full of: B. K. S. Iyengar *Light on Yoga* 47
I don't pretend: Graham Greene *Travels with My Aunt* 11
There is no: Leo Lerman *The Grand Surprise* 568
He has become: Ted Hughes *Tales From Ovid* 17
Drinking, unfortunately, can: Douglas Crase *Both* 206
Oh, dear, I: D. H. Lawrence *St. Mawr* 110
The measure of: Robert Frost *The Notebooks of Robert Frost* 315
But, dear David: Philip Roth *Professor of Desire* 128
"You wicked boy: Plato *Collected Dialogues* 107
Some time was: Albert Camus *The Plague* 148
"His wife is: Albert Camus *The Plague* 143
My eyes filled: Helen Keller *The World I Live In* 20
While his soul: James Joyce *Portrait of the Artist as a Young Man* 140
Even now, after: Kenzaburo Oe *A Personal Matter* 116
"He's living with: Kenzaburo Oe *A Personal Matter* 133
So I think: Lynne Sharon Schwartz *The Emergence of Memory* 45
Perhaps: Søren Kierkegaard *Works of Love* 234
And homesick is: James Blake *The Joint* 379
It was interesting: Don DeLillo *The Names* 265
What was his: Samuel Beckett *Disjecta* 63
He seemed to: Elizabeth Gilbert *Last American Man* 220
I remember everything: Fyodor Dostoevsky *House of the Dead* 320
I found his: Edmund White *My Lives* 248
"What do I: James Wood *The Book Against God* 248
There should have: Ken Kesey *Sometimes a Great Notion* 91
"I'm not recommending: John Francis Hunter *The Gay Insider* 56
"I couldn't do: Kenzaburo Oe *A Personal Matter* 127
"You are sleeping: J. M. Barrie *The White Bird* 209
"*I Love You*: Jonathan Ames *I Love You* 78
When God hands: Truman Capote *Music for Chameleons* xi
But not David's: John Waters *Role Models* 222

Rick Whitaker

"Well, I mean: Fyodor Dostoevsky *House of the Dead* 115
I segue into: Lydie Salvayre *Power of Flies* 2
Inconstancy, boredom, anxiety: Pascal *Pensees* 137
This estrangement is: John Koethe *Poetry at One Remove* 38
"I'll give you: Anthony Burgess *A Clockwork Orange* 74
"Now, just wait: John Cheever *Stories* 520
David beams, showing: John Waters *Role Models* 223
"I'm sure you: Christopher Priest *The Glamour* 169
But there he: Samuel Beckett *Disjecta* 50
What better way: Jacques Lacan *Four Fundamental Concepts* 133
"I wish you'd: J. D. Salinger *Franny and Zooey* 117
He was happiest: Gilbert Highet *Poets in a Landscape* 22
I watched them: Pamela Erens *The Understory* 16
Like lightning they: Giacomo Leopardi *Canti* 47
But what do: Julia Kristeva *Colette* 299
"Every son loves: Darcy O'Brien *A Way of Life Like Any Other* 25
One is inclined: John Koethe *Poetry at One Remove* 31
"He needs you: Andre Tellier *Twilight Men* 64
He could not: Gilbert Highet *Poets in a Landscape* 21
I thought of: Graham Greene *Travels with My Aunt* 19
We used to: Anne Landsman The Rowing Lesson 245
To the east: Warner *The Corner That Held Them* 10
But soon I: Anthony Burgess *A Clockwork Orange* 111
Why not: Craig Seligman *Sontag and Kael: Opposites Attract Me* 41

&ℭ 30 ℭℬ

I have returned: Umberto Eco *Mysterious Flame* 435
It's expensive, but: Charles Kaiser *The Gay Metropolis* vii
It has a: D. H. Lawrence *Etruscan Places* 8
The awareness that: Shunryu Suzuki *Zen Mind, Beginner's Mind* 40

188.

But nothing is: Sarah Bakewell *How to Live* 55

Everywhere I turned: J. G. Ballard *Miracles of Life* 29

Twenty-first century: Harold Bloom *Anatomy of Influence* 4

I refuse to: Rob Stephenson *Passes Through* 79

There, I always: Thomas Bernhard *My Prizes* 99

This clearer view: Harry Mathews *The Journalist* 4

"It's all very: Charles Dickens *Barnaby Rudge* 578

"Aren't you bored: Robert Walser *The Assistant* 233

He is rarely: Denis Donoghue *American Classics* 170

The older I: Anthony Holden *Tchaikovsky* 224

Love for a: Jean Genet *Funeral Rites* 18

A curious sea: Virginia Woolf *Diaries* Vol V 359

An atmosphere of: Giuseppe Tomasi di Lampedusa *The Leopard* 41

If I had: John Ashbery *Flow Chart* 29

A "feel bad": John Waters *Role Models* 171

Reading is like: Daniel Mendelsohn *The Elusive Embrace* 6

It was the: Susanna Pinney, ed. *I'll Stand by You: Letters of Sylvia Townsend Warner* 25

Climatically speaking: Jean Echenoz *I'm Gone* 189

Years ago I: Gore Vidal *Inventing a Nation* 7

You must admit: Georges Bataille *Blue of Noon* 34

"Ha ha ha: Afred Chester *Jamie Is My Heart's Desire* 101

She drained her: Graham Greene *Travels with My Aunt* 12

"I liked him: David Gilbert *Remote Feed* 116

"People can say: Jean Genet *Funeral Rites* 14

Adversity has its: Charles Kaiser *The Gay Metropolis* 218

The notion of: Emilio Lascano Tegui *On Elegance While Sleeping* 25

I am not: Umberto Eco *Mysterious Flame* 385

In other words: Alex Ross *Listen to This* 294

Mental confusion is: Georg Lukacs *History and Class Consciousness* xi

Human communication, it: Graham Greene *Travels with My Aunt* 84

Rick Whitaker

It's always late: Brane Mozetic *Banalities* 31
 "Want to guess: Dorothy Gallagher *Life Stories* 12
"What?" Joe said: Ken Kesey *Sometimes a Great Notion* 450
He lay back: Blair Niles *Strange Brother* 146
What does it: Daniel Mendelsohn *The Elusive Embrace* 51
"Her father," I: John Cheever *Stories* 684
We only laugh: Adam Phillips *Equals* 43
The youth became: Giuseppe Tomasi di Lampedusa *The
    Leopard* 27
"I met him: Graham Greene *Travels with My Aunt* 59
Unbearable: Samuel Beckett *Disjecta* 12
He kept asking: Alfred Chester *The Exquisite Corpse* 52
He says a: Truman Capote *A Christmas Memory* 72
I acted bored: Alfred Chester *The Exquisite Corpse* 53
To face up: Charles Guignon *On Being Authentic* 133
Funny, I'm not: Kenzaburo Oe *A Personal Matter* 131
What I need: Susanna Pinney, ed. *I'll Stand by You: Letters of
    Sylvia Townsend Warner* 8
It is a: W. G. Sebald *Vertigo* 157
And yet here: Bill Pronzini *The Hidden* 58
We are drinking: Truman Capote *Music for Chameleons* 3
Intellectually we were: Georg Lukacs *History and Class
    Consciousness* xi
The task would: Richard Wollheim *Painting as an Art* 301
How to avoid: Charles Henri Ford *Like Water from a Bucket* 36
Opting out of: Jean-Christophe Valtat *03* 65
Desire is the: Tim Dean *Unlimited Intimacy* 174
It is a: Lynne Sharon Schwartz *Emergence of Memory* 56
"Forget it, Joe: Ken Kesey *Sometimes a Great Notion* 475
Let's discuss you: John Francis Hunter *The Gay Insider* 35
But that didn't: Frederick and Steven Barthelme *Double Down* 135
"Efen if zey: Honoré de Balzac *Lost Illusions* 542

190.

Adultery's more fun: Green *The Heart of the Matter* 222

"So David tells: J. M. Barrie *The White Bird* 254

May we now: Joseph Breuer and Sigmund Freud *Studies in Hysteria* 164

Joe was not: Ron Padgett *Joe* 203

This the way: James Joyce *Finnegans Wake* 94

It was already: Anton Chekhov *The Portable Chekhov* 410

Full moon sends: Anne Carson *Autobiography of Red* 65

I wanted to: Denton Welch *Maiden Voyage* 284

I groaned and: Ken Kesey *Sometimes a Great Notion* 452

"I've got something: W. H. Auden *Forewords and Afterwords* 458

Love amazes, but: Susanna Pinney, ed. *I'll Stand by You: Letters of Sylvia Townsend Warner* 16

The most precious: Cather *Death Comes for the Archbishop* 38

"Not for long: Jenny McPhee *A Man of No Moon* 207

Joe listed one: Ken Kesey *Sometimes a Great Notion* 457

A dissatisfied mind: Henry James *Portrait of a Lady* 500

He wished he: Ted Hughes *Tales from Ovid* 33

"So is this: Robert Walser *The Assistant* 276

"I've had my: Sherwood Anderson *Winesburg, Ohio* 261

I don't know: Ray Carney *The films of John Cassavetes* 27

"No, freedom is: Anton Chekhov *The Portable Chekhov* 369

I think all: James Baldwin *Notes of a Native Son* 9

I took my: Evan S. Connell *Mrs. Bridge* 124

Finally, in all: Van Gulden *Real Parents Real Children* 221

"Oui, oui, c'est: Fyodor Dostoevsky *The Gambler* 82

He chewed, and: Thomas Bernhard *Frost* 23

Nothing is easy: Nick Piombino *Contradicta* 40

"Quietly, my son: J. M. Coetzee *Waiting for the Barbarians* 91

At eighteen minutes: J. M. Barrie *The White Bird* 114

"I am leaving: Warner *The Corner That Held Them* 20

"You must find: Warner *The Corner That Held Them* 21

Rick Whitaker

Nonsense: W. H. Auden *Collected Prose* Vol III 160
Non c'e peggior: Ilia Warner and Christopher Arnander *You
   Can't Get Blood Out of a Turnip* 90
No one is: Vladimir Lenin *State and Revolution* 46
I laughed in: Frank Lentricchia *The Italian Actress* 3
He was gone: J. D. Salinger *Nine Stories* 48
There remains only: W. G. Sebald *Vertigo* 154
Will our shame: Giacomo Leopardi *Canti* 53
It was all: Thomas Bernhard *My Prizes* 97

&? 31 ?&

But after all: Anton Chekhov *The Portable Chekhov* 340
The city and: Matthew Stadler *Allan Stein* 184
On one of: John Francis Hunter *The Gay Insider* 518
The mating of: W. H. Auden *Forewords and Afterwords* 518
With fallen branches: Kenneth Burke *Towards a Better Life* 27
The chords geese: Cotner and Fitch *Ten Walks/Two Talks* 10
Of all the: Karl Ove Knausgaard *My Struggle: Book Two* 61
"I believe Tarkovsky: Kenzaburo Oe *A Quiet Life* 86
He looked at: Harry Mathews *The Journalist* 54
I felt for: *Paris Review Interviews* Vol II 225
"My mother was: Charles Kaiser *The Gay Metropolis* 174
It was cooler: Patricia Highsmith *Tremor of Forgery* 146
I was never: Patrick White *Vivisector* 394
Some three years: Heinrich Kleist *Selected Prose* 269
Since then I've: Fyodor Dostoevsky *The Idiot* 56
It was a: F. Scott Fitzgerald *The Great Gatsby* 83
Encountering a stranger: Tim Dean *Unlimited Intimacy* 206
"Which reminds me: Robert Bolaño *Amulet* 45
Any congruence with: Jenny McPhee *A Man of No Moon* 151

On the high: Lucia Perillo *I've Heard the Vultures Singing* 28
Competition is a: J. M. Coetzee *Diary of a Bad Year* 80
This was disingenuous: Gore Vidal *Inventing a Nation* 109
"And I'm speaking: Truman Capote *A Christmas Memory* 57
Nevertheless, not everyone: Charles Kaiser *The Gay Metropolis* 264
Though I would: James Blake *The Joint* 275
To this day: Fyodor Dostoevsky *The Gambler* 161
In all my: Jean-Christophe Valtat *03* 71
And is the: Giacomo Leopardi *Canti* 87
Human sensitivity to: Pascal *Pensees* 14
"Would you please: Ernest Hemingway *Short Stories* 255
Nothing but disdain: Giacomo Leopardi *Canti* 89
The man with: Lydie Salvayre *Power of Flies* 102
As a boy: John Waters *Role Models* 177
Clearly the story: Kazuo Ishiguro *Remains of the Day* 36
He had a: Ellen Sussman *Dirty Words* 240
He has enormous: Jonathan Ames *I Love You* 97
But he never: Raymond Cooper *Bunk House Hunks* 115
He squeezes me: Amanda Michalopoulo *I'd Like* 77
The slow pressing: Paula Fox *The Coldest Winter* 55
You can feel: David Thomson *Have You Seen...?* 41
It occurred to: Pamela Erens *The Understory* 101
What is going: Edward Mendelson *Early Auden* 18
We're deep into: Harry Mathews *The Journalist* 23
"No," he said: Thomas Bernhard *Gargoyles* 51
I am, as: Vladimir Nabokov *Laughter in the Dark* 40
You should have: Kenzaburo Oe *A Personal Matter* 141
God approved his: Nathanael West *Miss Lonelyhearts* 57
"Yes, I know: Henry James *Portrait of a Lady* 403
No matter how: Nathanael West *Miss Lonelyhearts* 6
The man had: Thomas Bernhard *Gargoyles* 83
"No: Patrick White *Vivisector* 397

Rick Whitaker

Your Highness, I: Bertolt Brecht *Galileo* 93
The white American: James Baldwin *Notes of a Native Son* 119
"You have beautiful: Ernest Hemingway *A Farewell to Arms* 13
"Wait a second: Pamela Erens *The Understory* 141
A breeze was: Kazuo Ishiguro *Remains of the Day* 67
"You're not an: Ernest Hemingway *A Farewell to Arms* 18
That isn't funny: Bertolt Brecht *Galileo* 12
It was high: Sylvia Townsend Warner *Summer Will Show* 80
"Time to fuck: Christopher Priest *The Glamour* 166
Filth: it is: Milan Kundera *Testaments Betrayed* 47
Just how he: Justin Spring *Secret Historian* 160
Then for a: Joseph Conrad *Tales of Unrest* 34
My belly is: Alfred Chester *Looking for Genet* 57
To live beyond: Fyodor Dostoevsky *Notes from Underground* 7
But as I: F. Scott Fitzgerald *The Great Gatsby* 58
Eleanor, and only: Jane Austen *Northanger Abbey* 202
She was like: Jean-Christophe Valtat *03* 75
It was very: Henry James *The Europeans* 44
She looks as: Hart Crane *Library of America: Collected Poems and
    Selected Letters* 300
She was sort: Frederick and Steven Barthelme *Double Down* 68
"I don't know: Ronald Firbank *Three More Novels* 56
Not true: James Joyce *Portrait of the Artist as a Young Man* 177
She was cold: Warner *The Corner That Held Them* 28
Six years of: Warner *The Corner That Held Them* 29
"What are you: Alfred Chester *Jamie Is My Heart's Desire* 255
"My life lately: Gioia Timpanelli *Sometimes the Soul* 37
She put both: Fyodor Dostoevsky *The Gambler* 122
"You like being: Albert Camus *The Plague* 126
She is so: Edward Mendelson *The Things That Matter* 176
"You get along: Ernest Hemingway *Farewell to Arms* 19
"Oh yes," I: Christopher Priest *The Glamour* 206

Quite so: Plato *Collected Dialogues* 797

Cowed by my: Noel Coward *Pomp and Circumstance* 183

Her mouth was: Rachel Ingalls *Mrs. Caliban* 19

She was a: James Joyce *Dubliners* 102

I wanted to: Ernest Hemingway *Farewell to Arms* 25

I was elated: Fyodor Dostoevsky *The Gambler* 148

She wasn't sure: Darcy O'Brien *A Way of Life Like Any Other* 51

But we were: Frederick and Steven Barthelme *Double Down* 196

"You don't want: Christopher Priest *The Glamour* 203

She felt a: Jane Gardam *Faith Fox* 63

With an impulse: Craig Seligman *Sontag and Kael: Opposites
    Attract Me* 5

She wants to: Stephen Benatar *Wish Her Safe at Home* x

She had a: D. H. Lawrence *St. Mawr* 24

"Actually your father: Stephen Benatar *Wish Her Safe at Home* 5

In the darkness: Sylvia Townsend Warner *Summer Will Show* 90

All is mystery: Giacomo Leopardi *Canti* 115

We lust for: Ray Carney *The Films of John Cassavetes* 222

         ℬ 32 ℭ

Surprisingly, Eleanor journeyed: Marion Meade *Eleanor of
    Acquitaine* 266

And throughout the: Sylvia Townsend Warner *Summer Will
    Show* 117

From early morning: Herman Melville *The Confidence Man* 69

Those who thought: Herman Melville *The Confidence Man* 69

In short she: Filip Noterdaeme *The Autobiography of Daniel J.
    Isengart* 68

Rick Whitaker

❧ 33 ❧

The forsythia is: Pamela Erens *The Understory* 140

And you as: Samuel Beckett *Nohow On* 9

Do you remember: Frank Lentricchia *The Italian Actress* 7

I read again: Susan Sontag *Reborn* 12

To this end: Hart Crane *Library of America: Collected Poems and Selected Letters* 123

The pleasures of: Rachel Ingalls *Mrs. Caliban* 25

In the vicinity: Georges Bataille *The Blue of Noon* 19

The very writing: W. G. Sebald *Unrecounted* 8

"Language," says Wittgenstein: Marjorie Perloff *Wittgenstein's Ladder* 62

(Uttering a word: Ludwig Wittgenstein *Philosophical Investigations* 4

There is no: Ludwig Wittgenstein *Lectures 1930-32* 50

In short, all: Umberto Eco *Mysterious Flame* 364

For no reason: Georges Bataille *The Blue of Noon* 13

A writer without: Charles Burkhart *The Art of Ivy Compton-Burnett* 16

It's scarcely possible: Susan Sontag *Styles of Radical Will* 14

We are in: John Cheever *Stories* 532

A novel must: Charles Burkhart *The Art of Ivy Compton-Burnett* 17

"Once you pick: John Waters *Role Models* 95

❧ 34 ❧

Roy gets up: Dorothy Gallagher *Life Stories* 15

"Be sober," he: Gore Vidal *Inventing a Nation* 177

This succeeded, to: Franz Kafka *The Castle* 27

When he got: Justin Spring *Secret Historian* 164

That it should: William Shakespeare *Hamlet* (Yale) 22

He sat down: Henry James *Portrait of a Lady* 497

A bold, blunt-tipped: Willa Cather *Death Comes for the Archbishop* 31

Never as a: Paula Fox *Poor George* 28

He'd grown up: Edmund White *My Lives* 223

He gets up: Anton Chekhov *The Portable Chekhov* 310

So far so: Gore Vidal *Inventing a Nation* 82

"Every thing must: Edward Mendelson *The Things That Matter* 8

Don't be too: Samuel Beckett *Disjecta* 47

And he retained: Kenneth Silverman *Begin Again* 78

We came to: Joseph Conrad *Tales of Unrest* 15

He wrote a: Milan Kundera *Testaments Betrayed* 26

But is a: Milan Kundera *Testaments Betrayed* 11

We take almost: W. G. Sebald *Austerlitz* 134

He said one: John Cage *Musicage* 61

"You should write: Lydie Salvayre *Portrait of the Artist as a
    Domesticated Animal* 53

The most important: Richard Wollheim *Painting as an Art* 270

When I squint: Pamela Erens *The Understory* 75

The room was: AA Bronson *Lana* 152

Tell me, what: Giacomo Leopardi *Canti* 117

The policeman replies: Justin O'Brien *Camus* 85

I've only one: Henry James *Portrait of a Lady* 130

Fashion is very: John Waters *Role Models* 44

For this alone: Tony Judt *Memory Chalet* 87

I learned that: David Lynch *Lost Highway* xiv

We must learn: Kenneth Burke *Towards a Better Life* 9

The young man: Sylvia Townsend Warner *Summer Will Show* 108

Not bad, but: Emmanuel Carrère *My Life as a Russian Novel* 32

He would describe: Anderson Ferrell *Have You Heard* 5

His words sounded: Joseph Conrad *Tales of Unrest* 24

The style, as: Ray Carney *The Films of John Cassavetes* 189

Rick Whitaker

The Names of: James Joyce *Portrait of the Artist as a Young Man* 220
We stand at: Justin Taylor *Everything Here is the Best Thing Ever* 120
"Well, my very: Truman Capote *Music for Chameleons* 247
I wasn't in: David McConnell *Firebrat* 147
Must I remember: William Shakespeare *Hamlet* (Yale) 23
I ended by: Edmund Wilson *Axel's Castle* 216
Nothing contagious," I: Pamela Erens *The Understory* 13
Fictions constructed out: Susan Sontag *As Consciousness is
     Harnessed to Flesh* 513
"What is that: J. M. Coetzee *Waiting for the Barbarians* 142
There was salami: Patricia Highsmith *Tremor of Forgery* 239
"You said so: Alfred Chester *Jamie Is My Heart's Desire* 250
What foolishness!": Søren Kierkegaard *Works of Love* 288
His lips were: Franz Kafka *The Castle* 29
Enough, unhappy one: Giacomo Leopardi *Canti* 187

ℬ 35 ℭ

It was a: W. G. Sebald *Austerlitz* 142
Wild spring: James Joyce *Portrait of the Artist as a Young Man* 222
A pack of: Alex Ross *The Rest is Noise* 514
There was great: Willa Cather *Death Comes for the Archbishop* 41
I hated them: David Lynch *Lost Highway* xv
Yet they looked: Patrick Leigh Fermor *Time to Keep Silence* 13
It feels like: Jonathan Ames *I Love You* 110
It goes on: David Thomson *Have You Seen...?* 47
All night their: Sylvia Townsend Warner *The Corner That Held
     Them* 6
Let them howl: Vladimir Lenin *State and Revolution* 55
It is an: Iannis Xenakis *Formalized Music* 9
Perhaps it is: Tobias Schneebuam *Secret Places* 158

The telephone rings: Mikis Theodorakis *Journal of Resistance* 153
"Well, thank you: Philip Roth *Professor of Desire* 85
I'm tired of: Elizabeth Gilbert *Last American Man* 226
"It is essential: V. S. Pritchett *Dead Man Leading* 22
It is a: Ivy Compton-Burnett *A Family and a Fortune* 25
From tomorrow onwards: Honoré de Balzac *Lost Illusions* 556
It seems to: W. G. Sebald *Vertigo* 145
"Who is there: Raymond Cooper *Bunk House Hunks* 139
The police officer: J. M. Coetzee *Waiting for the Barbarians* 148
Again I had: Plato *Collected Dialogues* 559
"I'll be right: Alfred Chester *Jamie Is My Heart's Desire* 248
"But you're not: Alfred Chester *Jamie Is My Heart's Desire* 30
O Mary, go: John Ashbery *April Galleons* 19
"The arrangement," David: James Baldwin *Notes of a Native Son* 78
There was a: James Baldwin *Notes of a Native Son* 82
At dinner he: Rob Stephenson *Passes Through* 36
"And this guy: Charles Kaiser *The Gay Metropolis* 264
Huh?: Giles and Miller, eds. *The Arts of Contemplative Care* 77
"A poet, I: Virginia Woolf *Orlando* 80
It is two: J. M. Coetzee *Waiting for the Barbarians* 145
I have nothing: J. M. Coetzee *Waiting for the Barbarians* 48
What if you: Patrick White *Vivisector* 377
We belong to: Giles and Miller, eds. *The Arts of Contemplative Care* 138
I suffered from: Lydie Salvayre *Portrait of the Artist as a
    Domesticated Animal* 26
He tells of: Justin O'Brien *Camus* 95
"I did not: Colm Toibin *The Master* 41
Now at this: J. M. Coetzee *Waiting for the Barbarians* 150
That was the: Joseph Conrad *Tales of Unrest* 105
So I drank: Alfred Chester *The Exquisite Corpse* 54
The secret duel: Jorge Luis Borges *Collected Fictions* 292
Oh, how undignified: Karl Ove Knausgaard *My Struggle: Book*

199.

Two 44
"I have been: J. M. Coetzee *Waiting for the Barbarians* 144
The deepest history: Ray Carney *The Films of John Cassavetes* 140
The past is: James Joyce *Portrait of the Artist as a Young Man* 222
For an evening: J. M. Coetzee *Waiting for the Barbarians* 47

ᘒ 36 ᗷ

"It's because"—Joe: Ken Kesey *Sometimes a Great Notion* 462
He was leaning: Sylvia Townsend Warner *Summer Will Show* 113
As it happened: Tony Judt *Memory Chalet* 88
"God seeks people: Fyodor Dostoevsky *The Idiot* 81
Perhaps this willingness: Sarah Bakewell *How to Live* 56
 "I notice that: Willa Cather *Death Comes for the Archbishop* 31
It felt like: Edmund White *My Lives* 244
Youth is a: Thomas Bernhard *Gargoyles* 71
He has a: Rob Stephenson *Passes Through* 42
I turned away: Alfred Chester *Jamie Is My Heart's Desire* 30
I wobble a bit: Justin Taylor *Everything Here is the Best Thing Ever* 124
He was right: Anthony Holden *Tchaikovsky* 201
It is not: Fran Lebowitz *Reader* 11
Everyday life, with: Karl Ove Knausgaard *My Struggle: Book Two* 69
"To the Renaissance!: Nathanael West *Miss Lonelyhearts* 6
That sort of: Andre Tellier *Twilight Men* 24
"Just because it's: Ralph Sassone *The Intimates* 140
How many people: W. H. Auden *Forewords and Afterwords* 458
"Pah!" cried Joe: Charles Dickens *Barnaby Rudge* 26
There are perhaps: Marcel Proust *On Reading* 99
"And she ain't: Charles Dickens *Great Expectations* 55
Quoting gets on: Thomas Bernhard *Gargoyles* 78
Childhood seldom interests: Alan Bennett *Writing Home* xiii

Had he been: Christopher Priest *The Glamour* 44

He began to: Colm Toibin *The Master* 59

He felt ordinary: Sarah Bakewell *How to Live* 58

"Father," returned Joe: Charles Dickens *Barnaby Rudge* 25

But I reflected: James Wood *The Book Against God* 251

It is bewitching: George W. S. Trow *In the Context of No Context* 45

Aloud, I said: Thomas Bernhard *Gargoyles* 72

What I needed: Victoria Redel *Loverboy* 9

How I long: Susan Sontag *Reborn* 5

"How did that: David Leavitt *The Indian Clerk* 115

His mother is: Mikis Theodorakis *Journal of Resistance* 40

I couldn't have: Jenny McPhee *A Man of No Moon* 269

"Poor dear, you: Graham Greene *The Heart of the Matter* 49

She stared at: Paula Fox *Poor George* 107

"Don't kiss me: Sylvia Townsend Warner *The Corner That Held
    Them* 29

His voice had: Victoria Redel *Loverboy* 15

A sadist: George W. S. Trow *In the Context of No Context* 55

We were terrified: Tony Judt *Memory Chalet* 10

And suddenly he: Heinrich Boll *The Silent Angel* 140

He was obviously: Fyodor Dostoevsky *The Idiot* 78

"I don't like: J. D. Salinger *Nine Stories* 50

Joe felt there: Ron Padgett *Joe* 263

Our night had: Victoria Redel *Loverboy* 17

That time is: James Joyce *Portrait of the Artist as a Young Man* 181

"Oh, what the: J. D. Salinger *Franny and Zooey* 197

Is this a: Plato *Gorgias* 34

She powdered her: Jean Rhys *After Leaving Mr. Mackenzie* 40

"I have seen: Colm Toibin *The Master* 40

There she stood: D. H. Lawrence *Sons and Lovers* 337

On the other: David Thomson *Have You Seen… ?* 65

"Darling, I'm leaving: John Cheever *Stories* 497

Rick Whitaker

I feel kind: Jenny McPhee *A Man of No Moon* 171
He held out: Rudyard Kipling *Kim* 267
For hours they: D. H. Lawrence *Sons and Lovers* 23
Up and down: Sherwood Anderson *Winesburg, Ohio* 130
The Joe she: Jack London *The Game* 9
She refuses to: Janet Malcolm *Two Lives* 135
Whatever else is: James Joyce *Portrait of the Artist as a Young Man* 189

&) 37 (&

The remainder of: Gilbert Adair *Love and Death on Long Island* 126
I watched David: J. M. Barrie *The White Bird* 213
Oozing apple pie: Rob Stephenson *Passes Through* 40
In this large: David Lodge *Consciousness and the Novel* 92
But could I: Lydie Salvayre *Portrait of the Artist as a Domesticated
     Animal* 23
There was a: Ronald Firbank *Three More Novels* 60
That night I: Lydie Salvayre The *Power of Flies* 67

&) 38 (&

Roy was in: Dorothy Gallagher *Life Stories* 17
He said very: Joseph Conrad *Tales of Unrest* 123
He was in: Jean Cocteau *Holy Terrors* 129
He had barricaded: Thomas Bernhard *The Loser* 17
He told me: Rob Stephenson *Passes Through* 45
As is known: Fyodor Dostoevsky *The Idiot* 50
Love is the: Emilio Tegui *On Elegance While Sleeping* 42
On that note: Lydie Salvayre *Portrait of the Artist as a Domesticated
     Animal* 51

"Gimme a cigarette: J. D. Salinger *Nine Stories* 25

He was ugly: Giacomo Casanova *History of My Life* 989

There is nothing: Patricia Highsmith *Tremor of Forgery* 248

At least he: Gilbert Highet *Poets in a Landscape* 30

"I was once: Mary Jo Bang, trans. *The Inferno* 17

During the period: Georges Bataille *The Blue of Noon* 27

 "I think this: Colm Toibin *The Master* 249

How could anyone: Donald Keene *The Pleasures of Japanese
    Literature* 20

"Wake up and: Ralph Sassone *The Intimates* 93

Two or three: Umberto Eco *Mysterious Flame* 100

"Let me guess: Ralph Sassone *The Intimates* 87

Sometimes staying in: John Ashbery *April Galleons* 20

"I don't believe: Dorothy Gallagher *Life Stories* 18

I could hear: James Wood *The Book Against God* 252

She did not: D. H. Lawrence *Sons and Lovers* 41

The alert host: James Joyce *Dubliners* 86

"Is there anything: Andrew Holleran *Dancer from the Dance* 96

"If you would: Graham Greene *The Heart of the Matter* 228

I'll be brief: Danilo Kiš *A Tomb for Boris* 5

It's creepy, the: Rebecca Godfrey *The Torn Skirt* 140

"I am a: Geoff Dyer *Out of Sheer Rage: Wrestling with D. H.
    Lawrence* 40

"I'm doing a: Andrew Holleran *Dancer from the Dance* 144

Art, on this: Richard Wollheim *Painting as an Art* 246

The artist, like: James Joyce *Portrait of the Artist as a Young Man* 184

Excitement is muddling: Umberto Eco *Mysterious Flame* 298

"You'll succeed at: Ralph Sassone *The Intimates* 93

But isn't it: John Cheever *Stories* 497

Seated, she opened: J. D. Salinger *Nine Stories* 24

Next he showed: Albert Camus *The Plague* 135

It was difficult: Glen Baxter *The Further Blurtings of Glen Baxter*

Rick Whitaker

(no page numbers)

By now it: Sandor Marai *The Rebels* 5

"They never have: Andrew Holleran *Dancer from the Dance* 135

Frustration had been: Ralph Sassone *The Intimates* 141

As the evening: Glen Baxter *Atlas* (no page numbers)

Her mean, hunted: Georges Bataille *The Blue of Noon* 14

His waking hours: Edmund White *Nocturnes for the King of Naples* 130

I don't know: Anne Carson *Nox* (no page numbers)

We believe in: Ralph Waldo Emerson *Essays* 258

An hour goes: Rob Stephenson *Passes Through* 28

The rest of: Andre Tellier *Twilight Men* 80

That night, I: Lydie Salvayre *Portrait of the Artist as a Domesticated Animal* 26

&ivy; 39 &ivy;

I am teaching: Ted Hughes *Letters* 34

So far, so: Albert Camus *The Plague* 132

More or less: Frank Lentricchia *The Italian Actress* 39

I spent twenty-four: Giacomo Casanova *History of My Life* 928

I didn't understand: Brane Mozetic *Banalities* 16

Is this the: Emilio Lascano Tegui *On Elegance While Sleeping* 46

I was so: Lydie Salvayre *Portrait of the Artist as a Domesticated Animal* 50

Played the piano: Pyotr Tchaikovsky *Diaries* 25

"You can either: Adam Phillips *On Balance* 41

I remembered that: Edmund White *Jack Holmes and His Friend* 201

You had your: Sarah Bakewell *How to Live* 59

I ruminated for: Jean Genet *Funeral Rites* 17

Obediently the body: Christopher Isherwood *A Single Man* 13

I owe my: Giacomo Casanova *History of My Life* 944

That night there: Sylvia Townsend Warner *Kingdoms of Elfin* 197
White streets, white: Karl Ove Knausgaard *My Struggle: Book Two* 246
As I walked: Jean Genet *Funeral Rites* 12
Yes, I am: Guy Hocquenghem *Screwball Asses* 55
'Tis very strange: William Shakespeare *Hamlet* (Yale) 26
Homosexuality does not: Guy Hocquenghem *Screwball Asses* 55
Nothing is abnormal: George Orwell *An Age Like This* 12
Yes, but what: Plato *Gorgias* 13
To whom could: Roland Barthes *Mourning Diary* 213
It is when: Guy Hocquenghem *Screwball Asses* 47
Repression is a: Guy Hocquenghem *Screwball Asses* 23
One ages quickly: James Blake *The Joint* 89
There is a: Guy Hocquenghem *Screwball Asses* 55
This morning, more: Roland Barthes *Mourning Diary* 161
Parenthood, it seems: Michael Cunningham *By Nightfall* 169
Across the sky: Bruce Duffy *The World As I Found It* 31

ଯ 40 ଓ

The inquest concluded: W. G. Sebald *Rings of Saturn* 6

ଯ 41 ଓ

I got there: Giacomo Casanova *History of My Life* 964
They were waiting: Giacomo Leopardi *Canti* 317
The house was: Sylvia Townsend Warner *Kingdoms of Elfin* 197
I urinated, emitted: Diane Williams *The Stupefaction* 89
David's face assumed: E. F. Benson *David Blaize* 8
"Put me to: Honore Honoré de Balzac *Lost Illusions* 564

Does he think: Lydie Salvayre *Portrait of the Artist as a Domesticated Animal* 23

It was one: Lydie Salvayre *Portrait of the Artist as a Domesticated Animal* 174

"But, David, you: Sylvia Townsend Warner *Summer Will Show* 89

He got drunk: Giacomo Casanova *History of My Life* 988

He would never: James Joyce *Dubliners* 119

"I am a: Fyodor Dostoevsky *The Idiot* 81

You must yield: Giacomo Casanova *History of My Life* 1079

"Oh, damn!," said: E. F. Benson *David Blaize* 5

"—Suck it yourself: James Joyce *Finnegans Wake* 480

Sometimes when I'm : Justin Taylor *Everything Here is the Best Thing Ever* 118

But he must: Helen Keller *The World I Live In* 19

He himself repeatedly: Gilbert Highet *Poets in a Landscape* 181

Our entire reasoning: Blaise Pascal *Pensees* 124

At all events: W. G. Sebald *Vertigo* 6

ℊ 42 ℘

Joe was taking: Jack London *The Game* 67

"Say that I: Giacomo Casanova *History of My Life* 931

She depresses me: E. M. Forster *Passage to India* 131

He knew that: Jane Gardam *Faith Fox* 83

"Certainly not, it: Giacomo Casanova *History of My Life* 934

What were you: John Banville *The Untouchable* 196

Are you allowed: Franz Kafka *The Castle* 22

Why would someone: Adam Phillips *Equals* 73

"Why not," he: E. F. Benson *Freaks of Mayfair* 118

"What are you: Andre Tellier *Twilight Men* 29

"Goddam if I: J. D. Salinger *Nine Stories* 22

"It is a: Tim Dean *Unlimited Intimacy* 177

I should like: Daisetz T. Suzuki *Zen and Japanese Culture* 237

I can't find: Albert Camus *The First Man* 35

Exactly: Plato *Collected Dialogues* 117

I like it: Rob Stephenson *Passes Through* 30

And yet the: James Danziger *American Photographs* (no page
    numbers)

One who thinks: Shunryu Suzuki *Zen Mind, Beginner's Mind* 45

I never was: T. J. Parsell *Fish* 99

"What say you: Jane Austen *Northanger Abbey* 158

And where have: Ronald Firbank *Three More Novels* 148

She wore a: James Joyce *Dubliners* 119

She did not: Daisetz T. Suzuki *Zen and Japanese Culture* 224

She dealt with: James Joyce *Dubliners* 119

She reminded me: Lydie Salvayre *Portrait of the Artist as a
    Domesticated Animal* 175

I can see: Anne Carson *Nox* (no page numbers)

She stands on: George W. S. Trow *In the Conext of No Context* 59

History takes a: George W. S. Trow *In the Context of No Context* 59

She highly disapproves: Lydie Salvayre *The Power of Flies* 49

It began to: Patrick Leigh Fermor *A Time to Keep Silence* 12

Soon I will: Pyotr Tchaikovsky *Diaries* 27

Writing a book: George Orwell *An Age Like This* 7

I have not: Roland Barthes *Mourning Diary* 94

How often we: Roland Barthes *S/Z* xi

I love the: Anne Carson *Nox* (no pages numbers)

But if the: Herman Melville *The Confidence Man* 79

But I will: Herman Melville *The Confidence Man* 24

I would like: Guy Hocquenghem *Screwball Asses* 50

(Wilde speaks of: Roland Barthes *Reader* xxiii

❧ 43 ☙

David and I: J. M. Barrie *The White Bird* 267
We had been: W. Somerset Maugham *The Razor's Edge* 89
(Talking, talking: John Gardner *Grendel* 8
It seemed that: AA Bronson *Lana* 149
"This traffic jam: J. G. Ballard *Cocaine Nights* 11
Outside, the land: Italo Calvino *Invisible Cities* 14
"What seems beautiful: Charles Burkhart *The Art of I. Compton-Burnett* 66

❧ 44 ☙

Something lovely happened: Justin Spring *Secret Historian* 166
There was zest: Jean Rhys *After Leaving Mr. Mackenzie* 37
A policeman entered: Daniel Kehlmann *Measuring the World* 11
With a stick: Danilo Kiš *A Tomb for Boris* 9
Here he drank: Thomas Hardy *Jude the Obscure* 119
"Are you trying: James Joyce *Dubliners* 119
"I came here: Daniel Mendelsohn *The Elusive Embrace* 62
He bowed and: Jorge Luis Borges *Collected Fictions* 383
And that was: Thomas Bernhard *Frost* 11
And then there: Virginia Woolf *Diaries* Vol V. 359

❧ 45 ☙

Silence is a: Susan Sontag *Styles of Radical Will* 18
I have a: Jean-Christophe Valtat *03* 82

ℬ 46 ℭ

I am writing: Jean Genet *Funeral Rites* 13
And I'm still: Giacomo Leopardi *Canti* 21
Always alone: James Joyce *Portrait of the Artist as a Young Man* 196
This is a: Daisetz T. Suzuki *Zen and Japanese Culture* 232
I move books: Brane Mozetic *Banalities* 8
Our solutions are: Adam Phillips *On Balance* 272
Man has become: Guy Hocquenghem *Screwball Asses* 56
How did we: Giacomo Leopardi *Canti* 149
As the activity: Susan Sontag *Styles of Radical Will* 4
This is, as: Roland Barthes *Critical Essays* 12
The only good: Jean-Christophe Valtat *03* 48
It is endless: John Daido Loori *The Eight Gates of Zen* 44
Forget it; forget: Jean Rhys *After Leaving Mr. Mackenzie* 28
Zee End: James Joyce *Finnegans Wake* 28

ᨠ The Author ᨰ

Rick Whitaker is the author of *Assuming the Position: A Memoir of Hustling* and *The First Time I Met Frank O'Hara: Reading Gay American Writers.* He is Concerts and Theatre Manager of The Italian Academy at Columbia University, New York.